CW01335856

Wyrevale

The story begins

Conscience and reputation are two things.

Conscience is due to yourself, reputation to your neighbour.

Saint Augustine (354 AD - 430 AD)

That book is a work of fiction.

Any resemblance to persons living or dead is co-incidental

Participants

The Hamlets

- The Lakes
- The Views
- Devils Rise
- Brookdale
- The Abbey

The Residents

Amy and George	The Views
Claire and Richard	
Colin and Dina	
Roger and Nikki	Brookdale
Tony and Maria/Susie	
Jez and Megan	
Siobhan and Patrick	Devils Rise
Derek and Michelle	
Alex and Joan	
Michael and Suzanne	The Lakes
James and Paula	
Frankie – ex-resident	

CHAPTER ONE

The Party

Jeremy, Jez, was sixty-five. It was his birthday party and friends and neighbours had gathered round to celebrate the day. Thirty people had been invited to attend the house on the exclusive golf course development of Wyrevale. That green and pleasant living area had been constructed in the grounds of what was once an old Abbey, long since converted to luxury apartments, sufficiently situated in commuting distance for the major cities of Manchester, Chester, and Liverpool.

High worth individuals lived there so everyone thought. The material evidence was there to see. No one drove a Ford, unless it was a 4x4 or you were the teenage son or daughter, having just passed your driving test, grudgingly accepting the KA when the better skinned, more fashionable, Fiat 500 was your desire.

Mercedes, BMWs, and Audi cars were the norm. Jaguar and Porsche were common, and the number of Bentley Continentals would rival any Surrey stockbroker belt.

But beneath that layer, the reality was that the owners of such materialism were not necessarily what they seemed to be. The show could well have been built not on rock but on sand.

The appearance covered a reality which was not as glamorous as its outward look would have you believe.

In a gathering of that nature, the party, there are talkers and listeners.

Alex was a talker.

He liked to let those who would listen have the pleasure of his achievements. It is not uncommon amongst such individuals that the reality is warped to impress. He would be pleased to inform you of his fourteen million turnovers, his 23000 clients and the number of sales managers he had beneath him. That of course could all be true. It could also be a story which you were meant to take on board.

Frankie was a talker too.

The poor old donkey would have no legs when she was finished. She was not a resident of Wyrevale, but her ex-husband had been a member of the golf club, and her friendships established there had far outlasted her marriage.

Recently divorced, she was now a member of those ladies, the naughty forties, who were enjoying the new-found attention of male companions; to be polite. Frankie currently had a retinue of least four.

Derek was the clown prince or so you would have thought from his style of dress. Large baggy trousers in gaudy checks and multi coloured shoes, were his badge of office.

Derek would hold you spell bound on the minutiae of his current position in sales, for he had moved around quite a number of times.

It would have been paints whilst working for Dulux, Turkish delight from Cadbury, sausages at Walls or the current level of cornflakes at Kellogg's. If at all possible, care was taken to avoid initiating any subject which could be turned towards sales. If caught, your time would be held for much more than a few minutes.

George, on the other hand, could fall into the listener category.

A genuine successful man in his field with a worldwide executive position, he preferred to sit back and let others boast. He didn't have to do that. If asked he would tell you what he did, but in a way, that was much understated. Probably earning four times as much as anyone there, his success was evident from the Chichester built, Rolls Royce Ghost, in the drive.

Joan was neither a listener nor a talker. Joan was an attention seeker.

She would claim to be so tired from working. She worked from home selling garden furniture on the internet.

She would claim to have no money while booking exotic holidays; they of course were always a cheap deal or booked through air miles. All these tales in order to elicit the poor Joan response, but all around her knew of her ploys. Unfortunately for Joan her husband, Alex the unstoppable talker, would tell the truth, and inadvertently provide evidence to throw all her stories wide open.

Siobhan was certainly a talker; especially so once one bottle of Shiraz had been consumed.

Never shy of three bottles in a sitting, Siobhan was a drinker, a former resident of Liverpool. Her Irish background was ever present once alcohol had loosened the tongue. Molly Malone would have been proud. There would have been much fish sold on the market if she had Siobhan on the stall.

Siobhan was married to Patrick, whose profound deafness, a result of his former hidden identity, allowed him to live a quiet life as so much of her conversations went past him without being heard.

He tolerated her drunken episodes without a public acknowledgment of their existence. What happened behind closed doors no one knew. Whatever it was or was not did not curtail the next event, and it became accepted that if Siobhan was there, she would consume copious amounts of shorts, and Patrick, who rarely drank alcohol, would take her home before she fell down.

Michael was from Manchester and enormously proud of that.

His allegiance to Manchester City FC was legendary, and so was his hatred verging on paranoia, of the other Manchester team, name not to be mentioned.

Never one to hold back, Michael would say what he thought, never giving care to others feelings.

Michael was the anti-karaoke leader and would make it quite clear that he was not going to remain should that machine appear. His wife, Sonia, would be dragged away even if she was enjoying the moment. Sonia was a wife who was prepared to submit to the wishes of her husband.

Sabina was Jez's karaoke twin.

Sabina was also not a resident of Wyrevale but had gained access to the group by association with other members. She shared Jez's view that no good evening was complete without the intervention of the karaoke machine.

Heard once was not so bad, but time after time became a huge bore. The introduction of the machine was now a signal for many guests to leave. Sabina did indeed have a good voice, but Jez's repertoire was limited. "My Way" was his favourite. Sinatra would have turned in his grave.

Claire did not have to boast about her wealth, she had serious money.

That came by way of an inheritance from her father who had died when falling overboard on a transatlantic sailing race.

She devoted her time to her husband and children but had become obsessed with physical fitness. Many friends had told that her almost anorexic appearance was now too much and that a little extra weight would do her good.

None of that friendly advice was taken on board, and the daily ten kilometres she ran continued to increase the skeletal look.

Wyrevale development had been around for 15 years and consisted of hamlet groups of houses separated from each other by green field sites.

Each hamlet had its own character, and the use by the developers of different architecture, different builders gave the individuality that was sort out by those who chose to live there.

Each hamlet had its own name. Devils rise, The Views, Brookdale, The Lakes, were the given names. Each had its loyal following, and residents of one would easily find reasons for not living in one of the others.

Naturally, the higher priced houses were placed together and would appear to make that hamlet more exclusive. The Lakes claimed a special place, or though The Views, the bespoke houses, would make a serious challenge.

The group at Jez's party were spread widely around the hamlets, so individuals could be outwardly judged by their address, or so they thought.

Many were newcomers, which is to say residents for less than five years. Others would claim to have been the old guard having taken up their homes when many of the hamlets were yet to be built.

Siobhan would claim that at each opportunity and tell tales of how she had organised the creation of the Resident's Society. A society to which she no longer took part, for it had been taken over by wankers, her term, and was a waste of time.

Indeed, no one at the party played an active part in the Residents Society anymore, although there were those present who did actually form the nucleus of that emerging organization.

They also remembered that Siobhan was not what she claimed to be in that area.

As long as the newcomers were such, then no challenge would be made to her assertion by them. Those that knew would not rise to correct her either, it would be too embarrassing or would need a lot of clever manoeuvring not to cause harm to a particularly good friendship.

Roger was a listener.

His dislike for small talk, and his impaired hearing, obtained whilst diving in the

Caribbean, made his position in a very noisy circle critical if he was to contribute anything to the melee.

Distractions, such as background music, would keep him quieter than ever because not being able to hear what is said clearly, can make a response totally off the mark and be very embarrassing.

That role however, allowed him to pass a few hours watching and analysing; the people in the room would have no knowledge of that. He relied upon lip reading to understand most of what was said to him despite having spent a considerable sum of money on state-of-the-art hearing aids.

In a crowded noisy gathering such as one of the parties frequently held on Wyrevale, his keen eyesight could interpret the spoken word at many feet away.

Tony had an engineering background. His company had risen from small beginnings in a converted barn attached to his first wife's parent's farm. He produced replacement parts for the motor industry initially but had been one of the first people to recognise the value of 3D printing.

His engineering days were now over and with a move to a high technology business park; he had expanded the business using the new manufacturing method to his advantage. Unfortunately, his work dedication and an extremely attractive personal assistant had rapidly seen the end to the first marriage.

Currently living with Maria, who was not the assistant who caused the divorce, he still remained, even after eight years together, a man who was not content with life.

His passion outside of work was classic cars, of which he owned a rare light weight E-type Jaguar; one of only one hundred. He was still not a happy man, and without the classic car he kept for his entertainment, his home life had begun to bore him.

Unknown to Maria, but well known to every member of the party group, his current affair with Susie, was going strong. It was ironic that Susie was a Maria look alike, but had achieved that naturally, unlike Maria, whose looks owed much to the skills of a remarkably successful cosmetic surgeon.

On the outskirts of an industrial town with a history linked to heavy engineering, Wyrevale was a new breed of society. A society of the technological revolution, much of the wealth in the properties that populated the hamlets of the golf course came from IT.

The mobile phone revolution, the rapid expansion of computer users and the consequent software needs of the nation were all dealt with from within those four hamlets.

The covenants, of course, prohibited any use of the properties for business purposes, but those occupiers had no need for an office when the very business they were in, allowed them to work from home; convenient also, if the weather is good for eighteen holes and a round or two in the club house.

Golf can be the ultimate network game; many deals are concluded whilst riding a golf buggy. The game can also be fiercely competitive, with the handicap system encouraging a hierarchical boasting ritual.

"Do you play golf?"

"Yes"

What is your handicap?"

Anything in double figures would be met with hesitation, and if more than twenty, a complete conversation stopper.

Golf snobs abound, and there were many to be found on Wyrevale.

Jez, Derek, and Michael were golf addicts. Michael and Jez could make their low teens handicaps, but Derek would have you believe his low twenties was a mistake.

He could play better than that, but mostly in his mind. Occasionally, and only very occasionally, he would win the regular four some with Jeremy, a neighbour of Jez's.

Unfortunately, when that happened, anyone who would be within ear shot had the distinct pleasure of listening to the magnificent game that he had played. Often the story would be repeated throughout night.

Jez' s party was one of those nights, for Derek had won that day, and gathered here was a readymade audience to hear how it had been done.

"Two holes down after nine" he started "I got a two at the par three eleventh and couldn't go wrong from there"

The remaining members of that four would walk away as they had received the commentary whilst in play and couldn't stay to hear the embellishment that would be forthcoming. Derek found it easy to be economical with the truth.

The golf club had the potential to be the centre of social harmony, but poor management missed the opportunity to provide a decent restaurant service. Poor standards had reduced the number of residents who attended, to a small, dedicated number.

The obsessed golfers, however, would always be there after a round, denying their family lives, for golf is a very time-consuming game.

The Wyrevale course had been built to exacting North American PGA standards and at just over seven thousand yards was a long course. Throw in the distance between green and next tee, the round would take at least four hours, and on a competition day up to five and a half hours.

It is a very tolerant wife who can ignore that or one that was glad of the time to herself. Not a happy marriage then.

James had been in IT, where he worked for a large American software company.

His position was one of a trouble-shooter, being called in to manage projects that were stalled or looking bad. He had used that management experience to set up his own company selling cleaning products after sorting out the IT for a similar company in Devon and Cornwall.

His investigation of their business had made him realise the potential in that field. He had been a confirmed bachelor up to the age of thirty-five. That is until he met Paula, when James was on holiday in the Spanish resort of Marbella.

Paula was twenty-one and on holiday with her girlfriends. The group and Paula were dining at El Conti a fine dining restaurant set in the marina resort of Puerto Banus. Known for its seafood specialties, they had enjoyed the lobster special of the day.

James had been cruising the local establishments and had arrived at El Conti for a night cap, and whilst standing at the bar took note of the tall leggy brunette that passed by to the ladies.

As she returned, James managed to organise a collision whereby he spilt her drink. An offer to replenish the white wine was accepted by Paula who lingered to talk.

Three months later they were engaged and married within the year. That was 12 years ago, and now at 47, James spent many hours on the golf course, and more in the clubhouse.

Paula had an incredibly acceptable position working for Barclays Bank and ran their software development team from the national IT centre at Radbrooke Hall.

The nature of that job meant she too spent many hours away from their home. Despite Paula's senior Bank position, she was totally subservient to James's wishes.

If James said no, then that was a clear instruction to be obeyed. James, it seemed did not seem to reciprocate; he did what he wanted to do, regardless of Paula's feelings.

The mix of people were there to be seen at the party, not that that was any different to what might have been an impromptu evening following a round robin text to say that drinks were on offer over the weekend.

The ladies liked to drink bubbles, generally Prosecco and not champagne, since the discovery of a genuinely nice bottle available from Aldi. Although they liked to think they were a little up market, the volume that was regularly consumed made the judicious purchase from the German discounter necessary. It was a nice wine, having been voted top quality by the broadsheet press.

The mix of people had become familiar with each other for many years past, and it was rare that new members would join the group.

Anyone who had joined in the past had either been a new neighbour of one of the group or had been introduced via the golf club connection.

It was not always easy for them as newcomers to meld into the regular banter that had been developing, for the original members would have been together now for more than ten years.

There was one couple, however, who had made that transition.

Having originally lived in Wyrevale in the early 2000's, they had moved away to live in East Anglia, for the husband had taken a position at the University of East Anglia.

Colin lectured in musical composition.

Small, around five feet six with thinning ginger hair, his whole demeanour was one of a bygone almost hippy lifestyle. He would regularly travel to music festivals in the deep south of USA for his passion was the ukulele tunes of the Appalachian Mountain ranges. In the summertime he could be found in Northern Italy for the local guitar festivals around Lake Garda.

Dina, short for Geraldine, was Colin's wife, and a devout Christian. The sort of Christian that adorns their vehicle, nearly always a highly practical vehicle, maybe a Renault Kangoo, with that fish like symbol.

Given a few glasses of the Prosecco and the karaoke machine, she could become a local diva, belting out any tune in a not unreasonable soprano.

Any gathering at Colin and Dina's house would be full of music, for not only did they have the karaoke machine, but they also had the full amplification and sound mixing board to go with that.

Colin and Dina had moved back to Wyrevale when Colin had taken a position at a Mid-Cheshire college. He had viewed that as a rundown of his life towards retirement.

Dina was not entirely happy with that arrangement, but since her job role covered the whole of the country, a central home base was an advantage.

Dina was in charge of a large, cooled water distribution organisation, in which she could be called at any time to rescue a failed water cooler client.

Angel Falls was the name of the company, and she drove the company E-class Mercedes convertible.

Colin had a Ford Fiesta, maybe the only adult driven one on the development and that was exactly the level of his desired image. Theirs was not a happy marriage, and despite the outward appearance of all in harmony, the marriage was deeply troubled.

Dina had left before, and at Jez's party, Dina was recounting to the ladies how in one month's time she was moving again, leaving Colin behind. The Ford Fiesta had turned to bite him.

So, it was that the group around that glowing fire pit on a rapidly cooling evening, held between them a whole host of stories that had brought them to their new lives amongst the gentle rolling hills of Wyrevale golf resort and spa.

CHAPTER TWO

The Vale

The development of Wyrevale was conceived in the late 1980's, but the housing slump that developed at that time restricted the construction to just the conversion of the old Abbey into luxury apartments. These sold quite well in the beginning but at least four of the twelve remained unsold for many years.

The design for the golf course had been set out and several tee positions had been built during the apartment renovation, but when sales were not forthcoming, the course development was put on hold.

The original developers, Countywide, went bankrupt in 1988, and it was some ten years later that the project was rescued by Starwell Properties. They took a fresh look at the course design and made considerable changes, even abandoning many of the already built tee positions.

The changes reflected the new architect's desire to settle the housing groups as hamlets with green space between them. His concept was to use the natural surroundings to their maximum effect.

Set in the rolling hills on the border of the Cheshire plane, the position of the houses, now known as hamlets, was enshrined in their names.

The Lakes surrounded the water features which provided the challenge on the thirteenth and fourteenth holes. In total there were thirty-five houses in that group, and they were used as the signature group for the initial marketing campaign.

Construction had begun in the summer of 1998, with the show homes available for viewing from August 2000. At that time, the golf course was complete but would not be mature enough for play for a further two years. When a portion of the west wing of the Abbey was to become the golf clubhouse, complete with pro shop, locker rooms and function rooms.

Brookdale was the smallest of that hamlet development, if the exclusive Views were not taken into the equation, with only twenty houses.

As its name suggests the construction followed the course of the stream, the Chisel Brook, which had in times been responsible for carving out the valley from the native sandstone.

Set deep in the sweep between the hills the aspect of these houses was considered poorer than all the others, so the retail value of each was less.

The brook would eventually find its way into the lakes around which more prestigious homes were present, and then to flow onto the Dee estuary.

On each side, the first four and last two holes of the golf course did allow them to have an open aspect at the expense of some privacy as the golfers would pass by regularly on their carts.

The upper reaches of the valley, and from where the brook came, housed the old Abbey, the abundance of water supply had been a factor in its sixteenth century construction. Not only did it supply drinking water but gave the monastery a means of power for its flour mill.

The Abbey had seen many changes and had been at its height in the late nineteenth century but went into steady decline thereafter. At the turn of the century, 1900, the Catholic Church sold the then derelict buildings to a local industrial magnate who, with many additions, had converted it into residential accommodation.

Having made his millions from the local salt mines, Joseph Wyre was to lend his name to the current development. His children were not happy to maintain the Abbey after his death, so the offer from Countywide in1985, to purchase the Abbey and its surrounding parkland had readily been accepted.

Climbing out of the valley, the circular peripheral road would give rise to the third hamlet, Devils Rise.

Here the properties were set alongside the winding progress of the Parkland Road, which gave them varying, distinct aspects to the valley beneath and onwards to the lakes. Forty houses were set here, but because of their hillside position, the plots were of limited size, although the houses themselves were five and six bedrooms, some were three storeys.

The Views held prime position and contained the most expensive properties.

Ranging from one, to one point two million pounds, they were not the average homes, but had been built as bespoke dwellings at the behest of the original purchasers.

There were only fifteen in total, and each had a large, carefully landscaped plot to bring out the best in the natural hillside.

As their name suggests, the aspects of all gave them not only a view of the valley and lakes below, but onward to the mountains of North Wales and the Dee estuary. Many used large areas of glass in their construction to take advantage of the panorama that they had.

Many of the features of Wyrevale would use the American model of secured communities, and the entrance road contained 24-hour security posts, with bollard restricted entrance.

The security was maintained as part of the overall ground rent that each tenant paid annually. The rental also covered the grounds maintenance but not the upkeep of the golf course which was down to the club members themselves.

CHAPTER THREE

Roger

Roger had been retired for more than eight years from his teaching post in Dominica, and before that his very lucrative contract with the Government of Antigua and Barbuda had ended.

During the years there, with everything found by the Government he had managed to salt away a considerable sum, which now provided him a sufficiently high pension to lead a reasonably comfortable lifestyle.

When he had decided to move back to the UK, chose Wyrevale to be close to Manchester where his two children now lived. He had purchased a house in Brookdale in 2004.

He had started out studying microbiology at the University of Manchester in the early 1960's and graduated with a first-class BSc. His attention to detail in his studies lead to an MSc and PhD within three years of graduation, with his PhD thesis dealing with the effects and parasitic activity introduced to cattle by mosquito attack.

He moved from Manchester, where he lived with his first wife, Valerie, in a small, detached house in the suburb of Cheadle Hulme to the school of Tropical Medicine in London. There he could continue his research projects and translate his early work into the effects on humans.

Roger had met Valerie at University when she attended the weekly Friday night social events at the Students Union. Whilst not at university herself, she carried a student card from the secretarial college where she was studying.

Roger and Valerie became an item very quickly and for both of them that was the first true relationship that they had experienced, and with it the first venture into any form of sexual relations.

Neither of them had sufficient confidence on their own being to move away from what appeared to be a comfortable partnership during the twelve years they were together, but that outward appearance was false with a considerable number of underlying tensions.

On several occasions the link between them was only maintained by the family social pressures put upon them and the difficulty they felt they would have in explaining why it had failed.

With these false promises intact, they married shortly after Roger graduated for his BSc, when he was twenty-four and Valerie was twenty-three.

Far too young and far too inexperienced to contemplate that venture, they mistook being together for love. The marriage was doomed to failure from the outset but survived the 12 years with the production of two children,

Dominic, and Samantha, who would suffer greatly from the eventual divorce when they were 10 and 8 years old.

It would be many years later that Roger would discover the true nature of their complex feelings that had been generated by the split.

Although accepting that the family would have to move to London when Roger was offered the post at the School of Tropical Medicine, Valerie never really came to terms with the different social structures in place in the Southeast. She was a northern girl, for her parents still lived in Burnley where she was born and brought up.

As a true Lancashire lass, even the move south to Manchester to study had been a considerable upheaval.

As Roger took the post in London, she was again pushed into those realms of consciousness which were not easy for her to manage, and it was only with help from her local doctor who had prescribed anti-depressants, that she was able to travel south.

Roger was a truly dedicated researcher and put in long hours at the school. Coupled with these long hours, the nature of his research, which is tropical diseases, made him travel frequently to study the impact on locally resident populations. He was therefore away from home for extended periods of a time, and when at home came home late at night.

None of these things helped Valerie with her depression and Roger seemed completely unaware of her deepening dependency on the anti-depressants, and in-built insecurities. She had decided to take positive measures alone to find a way of occupying herself outside of that failing relationship.

She discovered that if she engaged herself in the activities of the children, and in particular their school activities she became calmer. So, it was that she was elected to the committee of the Parent Teachers Association of the school where they received their primary education.

The committee meetings would occur every month during term time and with Roger being absent for one reason or another, he did not count the number of times she attended.

Although there were genuine meetings, Valerie had struck up a relationship with one of the primary school teachers, and she and Alan, the teacher, began an affair which ran for over twelve months before Roger became suspicious.

Had it not been for the fact that Roger had caught an earlier flight back from Botswana, and arrived home half a day ahead of schedule, he would not have caught the two of them at home.

For the following 24 hours various recriminations were started as to why that situation had arisen, and why did Valerie need to look elsewhere when he, Roger, thought all was well between them at home.

During that discussion, it was revealed that Roger was no angel and that he had dallied beyond the marriage on more than one occasion.

When travelling abroad with attractive personal assistants, temptation can be hard to resist he was to claim. None of these one night stands however, had been more than sex for sex's sake, with never a suggestion of permanence in any of them.

Valerie and Alan, however, were now convinced that theirs was a genuine relationship and Alan was prepared to leave his wife and put his job on the line to make their affair a true and proper arrangement.

Roger was severely hurt by that but felt that he could not stop the rolling stone, so acted himself to put an end to their twelve-year marriage and sought a divorce.

Within 3 months they were living separate lives, and within 6 months Valerie had left and moved in with Alan, in a property purchased for her by her parents, and sufficiently far away from the London scene which she could not stand. The two children went with her as Roger could not be around for them in the job that he had.

Roger was left to fend for himself, and would live alone for the next two years, deeply involved with his research work, but increasingly finding that the newfound single existence was not necessarily easy to manage.

Visits with the children were arranged but it was becoming obvious that they had been disturbed by the divorce to a greater of lesser extent.

Dominic ,who was ten at the time of the split, seemed to accept the separation more easily than Samantha, who would breakdown at the end of each weekend visit, in fits of tears she would plead not to go back to her mother.

Practically, because of his job, the possibility of an eight-year-old remaining with him in London was not feasible. To explain that to his young daughter and to get her to understand that he was not rejecting her was extremely difficult and very upsetting for both parties.

The children were upset but no one knew how much the loss of them from his life had affected the inner being that lay deep within Roger's outward appearance.

Not a person who was openly emotional, the feelings ate away at him and in many a lonely night he would turn to the bottle of whisky, with at least half consumed before sleep took over. Many nights would pass with Roger waking around three am, fully dressed and still downstairs, with the bottle and empty glass beside him.

During the first eighteen months after the split Roger had tried to find new outgoings, as he was not a man who felt he could live alone. Three attempts at new relationships had failed. None of them lasted long, although during those times he was able to extend his previously limited sexual experience, something that previous one-night stands had not fulfilled.

His depression was spiralling down and over one holiday weekend it reached a depth that would see him not leave his bed for four days. It had to stop. With great will power he managed to drag his mind back from the edge, a suicidal edge, and strike out for new possibilities.

The Sunday Times that weekend carried an advertisement for a position in the Caribbean Island of Antigua. It was a government sponsored position dealing with the incidence of Dengue Fever in the Island; a fever carried by mosquitoes with which Roger was extremely familiar in his work at the School of Tropical Medicine.

He decided to submit his CV despite the fact that if he were to be given the position, he would further distance himself from the children.

The response took over a month to come back, with Roger almost giving up hope that his application had been accepted. When a response was received, he was invited to attend St John's, the capital of Antigua for an interview. It was the autumn of 1987.

His credentials were impeccable, matching the job specification exactly, so the offer to start in the position the following March was accepted without a backward glance.

Antigua and its neighbour Barbuda can be considered paradise islands, but the endemic mosquito population in the 1980's, and their effects on disease amongst the local population were a problem the local Government wanted to solve.

Rogers's task was to identify the type of mosquito responsible for the spread of the disease, its habitat and breeding grounds. His microbiological background gave him the ability to examine all aspects of the cause and transmission of the disease.

He would never truly solve the problem he was set but managed sufficiently to impress the people around him with his work ethic and capabilities that his presence in the islands was made permanent by the offer of citizenship in Antigua.

Roger had always felt that he could do better and become more involved with patients if he had a medical qualification, so after several years of working for the Government in Antigua, he applied for and was granted a place to study medicine as an undergraduate at Ross University Medical School on the island of Dominica.

Ross was set up in 1978 as a for profit University, and although it was deemed to accept medical students who had been rejected by the mainland schools in the USA, its graduates received sufficient education to obtain the American licence to practice in the USA.

Roger, because of his previous qualifications, was fast tracked through the course, achieving graduation in two rather than three years. He continued his post graduate studies at North-western University in Chicago. In line with his acknowledged dedication, he achieved resident status very quickly but opted to return to the Caribbean to proceed with work there that he felt was unfinished.

He did not return to Antigua however but accepted a teaching post at Ross where he had studied as an undergraduate. Ross University is situated in Portsmouth, the most northerly town on the Island of Dominica. It is one of the principal three towns, Marigot and Roseau the capital being the other two. Dominica, the largest of the Leeward Islands, proudly calls itself the Commonwealth of Dominica to distinguish it from the Dominican Republic.

Roger flourished in his new position and was soon heading for his own department of Pathology. His social life was vastly improved too and with the rugged terrain and primitive pot holed roads began a lifelong attraction to the Land Rover. An attraction he was to carry forward even on his return to the UK, with the preferred County Station Wagon over the much more elite Range Rover Vogue.

His romantic side had begun to reform, no doubt generated by the idyllic surroundings and sunshine, for at the age of fifty he met and fell in love with one of the nurses who worked in the hospital at Ross.

Nikki was nineteen.

CHAPTER FOUR

George

Of all the people at Jez's party, George was the closest to Roger. Of similar age, although George was the younger by six years, they had similar interests. At differing ends of the financial scale, Roger with the Land Rover, George with the Rolls Royce Ghost in the drive; Roger living in Brookdale, George on the Views, there was an underlying understanding between them that separated them from the general run of the social group.

George had started his career in the Royal Navy. His Father had commanded one of the destroyers that ran the convoy route to North Russian waters during the Second World War and was actively involved in the battle that saw the sinking of the German Pocket Battleship Scharnhorst in the North Atlantic.

The Navy was a tradition in George's family, and it was expected that George would follow the family line. Born and bred in Portsmouth, the Naval Dockyards were just a stone's throw away from the family home. So, in 1969 at the age of eighteen, he gave up the chance to go to university, and enrolled at Dartmouth Naval Academy.

His background, family connections and devotion to the Senior Service stood him in good stead. On leaving the Academy three years later, a Sub-Lieutenant, he was given a shipboard posting almost immediately. His career spanned duties in the Arabian Gulf, the drug patrols in the Caribbean and promotional trips around the world.

His ship, on which he was second in command, saw action in the Falklands war, and was lucky to escape the air attack on 24 May 1982 in San Carlos Water on the Fleet Auxiliary Sir Galahad, as she was attacked by A-4 Skyhawks of the Argentine Air Force's IV Brigade Aérea. Sir Galahad would be later destroyed while unloading Welsh Guards in Port Pleasant, off Fitzroy, with such tragic loss of life.

At the age of forty-seven, he had risen to Captain of a type 45 frigate at which point he decided that he wanted a change of direction. At his age he was able to leave the service with a sizeable pension, but George was determined not to sit on his laurels and become a businessman.

Back home in Portsmouth, he setup his own computer business, for his Naval career and training had introduced him to that innovative technology incredibly early in the 1980's and his interest and available knowledge had led him to a considerable expertise in that field.

He had met his wife shortly after leaving Dartmouth College and they had married when George was twenty-four and Amy, his wife, was twenty. She too had a family background based around the Naval institutions of Portsmouth.

She had been a civilian attached to the large Naval base, HMS Nelson. Her work was to bring her into close contact with the new Sub-Lieutenants on a daily basis, of whom George was one. Their mutual attraction was immediate, love at first sight, and they would spend much time together prior to his first shipboard posting.

Amy was to accept the long absences and worry when George was at sea with good grace and the arrival of their first daughter, Lisa, gave her much to occupy her, especially when daughter number two, Polly, arrived within two years. So much for the brief home time from sea that was responsible for these two early conceptions.

Amy's independent lifestyle was supported well by her devotion to the family and the spiritual support she received from the local Evangelical Church.

She had started attending when the girls were old enough to go with her and could join in the rousing anthems sung there each Sunday. The devotion to the Church was to follow her throughout her life, and with a spirit of community service, giving much of her time to voluntary work, initially with the elderly residents of the Naval Retirement Homes.

George and Amy had been married for 38 years and their current lifestyle could not have been better. George's business had spread its wings into providing software for the military; an easy step, for that was the base from which it had grown.

George had the knowledge of requirements from his various assignments and the company soon attracted the interest of the American Military suppliers; so much so that after only a brief time supplying them, he was able to sell off the company to a subsidiary of General Motors and turn his head to new projects.

He had seen the value of computer aided and guided military hardware and was now keen to enter the field of robotics. General Motors had kept him on in a consultancy position, following the purchase of his company, so through that he was able to get access to robotics in the automotive industry.

That field had a worldwide appeal, and it was not long before he was head hunted by the Japanese company, Toyota whose presence in the world marketplace was ever growing; with Detroit in decline, George was quick to accept their offer, particularly now that he could keep his UK base.

It did however mean moving North as Toyota were establishing their British Base near Derby in the East Midlands. The company assisted in moving and house provision, allowing George and Amy to benefit from the sale of their southern base.

The two daughters were soon to leave home to attend University. Lisa the oldest of the two would study Media at St Andrews in Scotland, whilst Polly, the younger would take an opportunity to use her father's connections in the USA to study at North-western University in Chicago.

Lisa obtained her first job with the BBC, initially as a production assistant and moving up to producer of art/history documentaries out of the BBC Northern Headquarters in Oxford Road, Manchester.

Polly had spent three years in Chicago with her American Studies but had failed to find a niche in which to use her degree and had returned home to live with her parents. Her time in the States had however given her a taste for travel and she would dabble with the tourist Industry in both travel agent form and air crew, finally settling for an overseas posting with British Airways as one of their representatives in the UAE.

It was Lisa's position in Manchester that attracted George and Amy to move to their Cheshire retreat on George's retirement, and with the profits they had achieved by the sale of their property in Chichester on his move with Toyota. They were easily able to purchase outright the house on the Views, which was on the market for £750,000, considerably less than the £1.2 million they had received from a sailing stockbroker, looking for a weekend getaway from the City of London. T

The house they left behind had its own mooring, and a yacht could be brought alongside. They had purchased the large property overlooking the estuary in Chichester when George had sold his first company many years before, rising prices and the sailing attractions of that area had made their purchase an excellent investment.

George had a long-standing problem with his health, for he had been diagnosed with type 2 diabetes whilst still a serving officer and had been closely monitored during the latter years of his Naval career.

Now, as a civilian, it was down to him alone to keep a check on his health, so his keep fit regime and calorie intake were paramount in his lifestyle. Daily insulin injections had been able to keep blood sugars under control, but he felt that he had to maintain a high degree of general fitness. The daily run around Wyrevale or out on his racing cycle were paramount.

His worldwide position in the company and its incumbent long-distance air travel also made him conscious of his fitness levels. He never ever booked himself into a hotel which did not have a gym, for he substituted his daily home routine for the treadmills, getting up, if necessary, at 5am to have sufficient time to exercise.

Amy, with her history of community service in Chichester, had to find new outlets on arriving in Wyrevale. That she did by joining the parish council. She no longer had the evangelical church behind her, but the local church Sunday services were enough to keep her in touch with her spiritual needs.

Amy wore tweeds and was very traditional in her outlook. The twin sets, sensible shoes, and devotion to the Conservative Party, were all part of her make-up, yet she was never shy of the social occasions that were part of the life in Wyrevale.

Her daily life however was spent almost entirely at home, where she would devote long hours to cleaning and solitary exploration of the internet. Her outward show of wealth was muted; her clothing, her shoes, and the ten-year-old car she drove were classically her idea of playing down the large financial base that she and George enjoyed.

CHAPTER FIVE

Summer Ball

The residents of Wyrevale were never shy of a charitable event. Maybe in some way that was a means to satisfy an unconscious feeling of guilt for their wealth and apparent rich lifestyle.

The first such event after Jez's party was the annual summer ball at the golf club, held in the function room upstairs. Away from the bar with its 19th hole drinking golfers, the room was big enough to seat 150 on tables of ten, with sufficient room for a small dance floor in front of the raised dais which served as a stage.

Usually, the music would be provided by a DJ from the local township, but on special occasions such as that, a live band would play. That year, the seven-piece ensemble was called the Bluetones, with their mixture of jazz, rhythm, and blues.

George and Amy were always the first to book a table and would choose to inhabit that with Jez and Megan, Roger, Nikki, Claire, and Richard. The fifth couple would always be a problem to find, for the original eight were close friends and would often dine at each other's houses. The last two members of the table would never be the same as different couples would be tried out at each event.

For the summer ball that year, the couple invited were Alex and Joan, as Richard had business connections with Alex and Joan would occasionally lunch with the ladies.

Alex was a complex character. He had the natural presentation of a salesman, loud, talkative, and known to embellish much of his conversation with the superlatives that are required to clinch sales.

Alex was forty-five, but looked older, as the greying hair and developing bald patch had compromised his looks. He owned his own company in Widnes and had started that with his brother in their late teens when the IT industry was in its infancy.

They would buy all the parts from Radio Shack and assemble their own circuit boards from which home computers would be formed. In the early 1990's personal computers were not fully established and even Microsoft was a small company trying to establish itself as a dominant force in the operating system marketplace.

DOS had become windows and Alex and his brother were able to translate to these new fields very quickly, but the development software was racing ahead leaving them behind, so they decided to concentrate their business on hardware platforms.

Their initial success brought them a good deal of money very quickly and although Alex was already married, his brother was single.

Brother John would choose to spend his money on fast cars, and it was on one fatal day in February 1995 that his Jaguar left the road on the Macclesfield/Buxton Road – Cat and Fiddle pass, that John lost his life.

Alex, the younger of the two brothers was left the business to run and a big hole in his emotional life; a hole which had great bearing on his personal development going forward.

John as the senior member of the business had always been allowed the financial control of the company and what Alex was to discover on his death, was that the business was in severe financial difficulties. The rich lifestyle that John had enjoyed, the fast cars and exotic holidays had come at the expense of the business. Much of the funds were drawn direct from the business account without reference to Alex.

Coping with sudden death was bad enough, and the realisation that his brother had let him down, in business and personally, threw Alex into a deep depression; that would not leave him for many years to come. Only with the help of counselling and the support of Joan would get him through it.

It was a matter of starting all over again, and what was once a thriving business had to reinvent itself in the unfamiliar environment to become viable once more.

The rise of low-price manufactured computers made the construction of their own machines no longer acceptable to the marketplace and Alex had to discover a new area of expertise in which to drive the company forward.

Although his simple circuit boards were no longer sufficiently sophisticated to power the ever-increasing complexity of personal computers, Alex discovered that they could easily be adapted to power small electronic devices; smoke alarms, doorbells, burglar alarms and electronic timers all fell within the range of his company's products.

Alex had been the sales force of the old company and it was in that capacity that he set out to market these small devices. From its low base, the company steadily grew, and when he obtained a large contract to supply chain of DIY stores in the Northwest of England, the company began to return to profit.

During the struggling 5 years after John's death, the bread was maintained on the table by Joan. She had a small retail outlet selling interior decorations. That, with Alex's work schedule put the prospect of children out of the question, and it was said that the absence of children in their lives had been a conscious decision.

In reality, Alex's depression and its effect on his libido were the main cause. That was revealed one day by Joan, who on a wine filled Ladies Day at Chester Races had told her group the truth, many of whom were now sat at George and Amy's table.

Alex's libido and tendency to premature ejaculation had led to their marriage becoming sexless and Joan was extremely happy to state that they had not had sex in the last ten years.

Unfortunately for Joan, Alex in his cups would become quiet feely, touchy and to her and all those present, embarrassing.

Knowing what they did, for wives cannot keep such ripe gossip to themselves, willingly sharing such with their husbands, made his behaviour all the more disgusting.

The combination of alcohol and antidepressants is not a good one. Joan would also attribute his behaviour to the presence of a full moon, for if it can affect the tides, why is it unreasonable to think that mood swings can be affected in a vulnerable individual like Alex.

Alex's business did not help is state of mind, for although moderately successful, their household mainstay was now Joan's blossoming internet connections.

Joan, whose interior decor shop survived the years, was one of the first to recognise the power of selling on the internet and now had the internet shop selling imported teak furniture from Indonesia.

To that end she had purchased a Mercedes Vito van to transport her goods and a small warehouse for her stock and distribution centre. Her neighbours in the Lakes were not keen on the logoed vehicle being parked in her driveway, for it breached the local covenants which applied to Wyrevale.

They would much prefer to see her neat Mini Cooper S convertible, which suited Joan at 5ft 2in in height, very well. Joan had indulged Alex, despite bad memories of his brother's death by purchasing for him a Jaguar XF.

The summer ball raised money for a local hospice through ticket sales and auctions that took place at the end of dinner.

Donations of prizes for the auction were always sought and to some extent there was a degree of rivalry amongst attendees not only in the bidding, but also in the original supply of the items to be auctioned.

In the past, George with his international connections had been able to secure trophies from sporting events worldwide; an England cricket bat, a rugby ball from New Zealand and a Formula One paddock jacket courtesy of Toyota.

That summer he had been unable to bring anything to the auction, so he was to be out shone by Jez who, with his boxing connections, had managed to obtain a pair of shorts worn by Henry Cooper, admittedly only in training, when he fought and nearly beat the then named Cassius Clay, shortly to become Muhammad Ali.

A prize which only the over 60's present would recognise. Consequently, the amount raised disappointed Jez and took the shine off his donation brownie points.

The summer ball that year succeeded in raising £5320 for the local hospice, and every one present was able to return home with the feeling that they had been part of socially agreeable occasion.

Alex was to suffer the most monumental hangover, which in no way helped his depression. The rest of the guests at George and Amy's table had yet more gossip to be discussed when they next met, as Alex had succeeded in crowning the evening falling on the table and knocking glasses and wine bottles across the room.

Joan hurriedly collected him and left early under a cloud, leaving the others to wonder how she managed to live with him.

Jez took the lead after Alex's departure and tried to cover the event by encouraging everyone on to the dance floor, much to Roger's regret as he was not at all inclined to participate. Nikki on the other hand, with her Caribbean background would dance the night away if she could, with that characteristic loose-limbed action that can be found on all the islands.

The night was to end at 1 o'clock, and all were able to saunter home without worry of drink driving rules as no one lived more than a mile from the clubhouse, and none had to leave the private roads inside the gated development.

CHAPTER SIX

Jez and Megan

Jez and Megan were an interesting couple, with such a catalogue of events in their history that a separate book could be written about them.

Jez had grown up in the East End of London in those tough times when the place was ruled by the Richardson Gang and the notorious Kray Twins were about. Jez had followed in his father's footsteps with a keen interest in boxing, winning several bouts as an amateur before turning professional at age eighteen.

He competed regularly and was often on the bill at Shoreditch Town Hall arena. His training was conducted in the back-street gym his father had set up when his own ring appearances were in decline.

Although successful as an amateur he struggled in the professional ring and on many occasions, he had to try extremely hard to make the fighting weight. Over the years those fluctuating weight problems were never to go away.

A Father himself at age 19 and married with two children at 21 his life was typical of the tough East End streets. His early minor successes brought him into contact with the prominent underworld figures, and when his boxing days were over, he functioned as security for many of the gangland bosses.

The chosen profession brought with it various visits to high society places in London that the underworld would frequent, and in the 1970's one of the most popular was the Playboy club, with its Bunny Girl hostesses.

Bunny Girls were an invention of the eccentric boss of Playboy, Hugh Hefner and they had a strict code of conduct right down to the exact shape and dimension of the bunny outfits, which were individually padded in appropriate places to give the desired curves required. There were strict rules to how to deal with customers and learnt the 'bunny dip' to deposit drinks at customer tables.

One such girl, and erstwhile University Student, who was moonlighting, was Megan. Jez was to meet her on many occasions on his nightly visits, but rules prevented them from meeting socially, and besides Megan considered that young gangland enforcer as off limits and married in any case. It would be many years before they would meet again.

Megan succeeded in obtaining, despite her moonlighting; a second-class honours degree in business studies and left University with little or no idea as to how she would pursue her career.

An article in the Sunday papers attracted her attention, setting out the idea of life on a cruise ship as a member of the crew. She applied and was taken on by a minor cruise liner as the purser for the next round the world trip.

The cruise would take them south from Southampton, round Cape Horn into the Indian Ocean and onward across the Pacific calling at many of the small exotic South Pacific islands.

Megan had a riotous time on board; only when returning to the UK did, she discover that her bar bill exceeded the wage she was to be paid. Trapped in that position she was forced to sign on again to pay off her debt, and that time she was to be more abstemious.

Coming ashore after that second trip, she realised that the party lifestyle was not going to last forever, and she would need to find position which would supply her with all her daily needs.

Further education was considered the way to move forward, and with the small sum she had managed to retain from her last cruise, she put herself through a management training course which led her into working in public relations.

Ten years down the line from that decision, she had established her own public relations company which was quickly making a name for itself in and around London.

During that ten-year period, Jez had taken on the running of his Father's gym and given up his security position with the gangs of the East End, many of whom were either in prison or had been murdered by their fellow or rival gang members. The Met had begun to deal with organised crime with both the Richardsons and the Krays brought to justice.

His interest and knowledge of training gave him an advantage when he decided to expand his company by purchasing local gyms, and with the money he had accumulated in his previous position being readily available and the coming interest in keeping fit, he was one of the first people to realise that there was a market to exploit.

His company after ten years was growing fast, and he needed to shrug off the East End criminal background so that he could strike out into more affluent areas of suburbia where the interest in keeping fit was strongest.

To that end he set about finding a PR company to represent his interests, clean up his image and present a new face especially to the money men in the City of London. By chance he was to choose Megan's company to represent him.

Meagan recognised him immediately on their first meeting, as the young tough guy from her Playboy Club days, but Jez would not make that connection for many months working together. Now at the age of thirty-five his marriage was having difficulties, and his wife, Mary had begun an affair with one of Jez's clients who was currently a champion body builder.

Jez, who had been preoccupied for many years with the expansion of his company, had not seen that coming, but it was on holiday in the South of France near Cap D'Agde that his senses were alerted, when 'by chance' the man in question was on holiday at the same resort.

Mary made the mistake of giving the body builder too much attention around the pool and the body language spoke a thousand words.

After their first week away, and following a violent argument, fuelled by an excellent burgundy, Mary confessed to the affair of two years standing. That was enough for Jez who had been struggling to keep their marriage together, and he decided to call it a day.

On their return to England, Jez placed the marital home on the market, and contacted his lawyer to begin divorce proceedings. His relative financial position was such that he was able to pay Mary off and still manage to live in the manner to which he had become accustomed, but now as a single man.

His newfound independent means allowed him to follow a pathway of his own making. The two children he had with Mary were in their late teens and well catered for in the manner that only private education can give. His relationship with them would take a step back but as they grew older and more endowed with life experience they would come back into his life.

During the first two years of separation from Mary, and following the completion of the decree nisi, Jez had several abortive relationships; each having a life cycle of no more than a few months. During that time, his working relationship with Megan was flourishing as his company expanded into a large chain of fitness centres throughout the Southeast and East Anglia.

Megan's company had managed to dispel all the connections to Jez's early lifestyle and underworld connections and their success brought more contact between the two of them. An unlikely looking couple, Jez at six feet two, with the ponytail now showing many signs of grey; Megan of typical Welsh stock, five feet two and compactly built.

To celebrate the opening of the 25th Centre, Jez had invited the top employees from Megan's company to his villa in Southern Spain.

He had purchased the villa on the prestigious La Zagaletta development when the Costa del Sol was a haven for the underworld figures and had managed to retain it during the divorce proceedings with Mary.

His keen interest in Golf had steered him there as it had an exclusive club and in time would add a further course for its residents. Business colleagues would regularly visit and enjoy the facilities offered by that villa with its luxury amenities.

The villa could sleep ten people, had a gym, a cinema room, large outdoor pool, and a fantastic view down the valley to Estepona. Being only twenty minutes away from the resort of Puerto Banus was an added bonus, and ideal for corporate entertaining.

His invitation to Megan's company was not readily taken up, but Megan herself said she could spare a long weekend from her busy schedule in August. Megan had never married but had a long-term relationship with David whom she met during her early days in public relations, with a minor contract at the BBC. David was a radio producer for Radio 4.

Her ambition to strike out on her own had not gone down well with David, and the success she had achieved put a considerable strain on their relationship for it took her away from him a lot and he was an individual who was very needy, requiring a good deal of open affection and attention. He was therefore not keen to see her take that break without him, hence Megan's desire to restrict the visit to just a long weekend.

The flight from Gatwick to Malaga was scheduled to land at 11.20 on the Saturday morning and Jez had arranged transport to collect her for the forty-five-minute drive south to La Zagaletta.

He was unable to make that personally as he had other guests staying and would be on the golf course at 8am that day. The driver, who collected Megan, had been instructed to deliver her to the Golf Club where she would meet the group for lunch and from there, Jez could personally introduce her to his villa surroundings.

Megan was unaware that the Golfing group were scheduled to leave the following day, leaving just Jez and herself in the villa. It was over the next three days that they both realised that a long term, but distant attraction had been present for many years; in fact, Megan would later confess to Jez that she had fancied him right from the first encounter way back in her Bunny Girl days.

The sun, the villa and the nearby availability of high-class restaurants made for a very romantic setting and their relationship was sparked very quickly.

On her return to London, Megan had to deal with the David problem, and Jez's return would complicate that further. His constant phone calls, invitations to dinner, concerts and corporate events were difficult to resist now that she knew of his feelings for her. Showered with red roses she just had to come clean.

By December of that year, Jez and Megan decided they had to speak with David and move in together much to his annoyance. He did not let go easily and would plague Megan for several months after in the hope she would return. She did not and Jez finally asked her to marry him one year later whilst on holiday in the Maldives. Not a huge occasion, the wedding with a few close friends in attendance, was conducted on a beach in Mauritius in September 1995.

Megan was of Welsh stock, having left home in Rhyl on the North Wales coast to attend University in London all those years ago. Now with their joint successful businesses they were able to choose any place in the country to live, and when Jez found a buyer for his chain of leisure clubs, they decided to move north so that Megan could be closer to her relatives in Wales. They had purchased the best plot on Devils Rise with a view down the valley as good as that of the bespoke houses on the Views.

On his retirement at 55, Jez increased his passion for motor cycling that he had nurtured whilst a single man after separating from Mary and could often be seen setting off on his Harley Davidson for a leisure ride through North Wales and return via Snowdonia.

He had accompanied that passion by allowing his greying hair to grow into a ponytail and maintained a well-manicured goatee beard.

Motorcycles have a distinct attraction to certain types of men, and amongst the residents of Wyrevale, Jez would have a like-minded biker in Patrick.

CHAPTER SEVEN

Patrick and Siobhan

Patrick and Siobhan had not attended the summer ball that year, as they were extremely disappointed with the quality of the food served on the previous occasion.

They were Irish but had lived in Liverpool for many years, or so they said.

Patrick and Siobhan were not their real names and they had in fact moved to Wyrevale from Bristol where Patrick had run a successful motorcycle franchise which had been given to him under the Government sponsored witness protection scheme.

Their move to Wyrevale was one of many that they had to have since their escape from the troubles in Northern Ireland.

Patrick was a Protestant from Belfast and Siobhan was a Catholic from Ballina in County Mayo in the Republic. In his youth, Patrick had been a member of those uniquely Irish phenomena, the Show Band and had toured the South in that manner. Siobhan had met him when they performed at the Pump House, a venue alongside the river Moy which flows through the town.

Back in Belfast, Patrick's family had become members of the UDA, the Ulster Defence Association; the Protestant militant organisation that campaigned for the retention of protestant majority rule in Ulster (Northern Ireland).

The Ulster Defence Association was the largest Ulster loyalist paramilitary and vigilante group in Northern Ireland. It was formed in September 1971 and undertook a campaign of almost twenty-four years during The Troubles.

Within the UDA was a group tasked with launching paramilitary attacks; it used the cover name Ulster Freedom Fighters (UFF) so that the UDA would not be outlawed. The United Kingdom outlawed the "UFF" in November 1973, but the UDA itself was not classified as a terrorist group until 10 August 1992.

The UDA's/UFF's declared goal was to defend Protestant loyalist areas and to combat Irish republicanism, particularly the Provisional IRA. However, most of its victims were unarmed civilians. The majority of them were Irish Catholics, killed in what the group called retaliation for IRA actions or attacks on Protestants.

It is easy therefore to imagine the strain that was pit on the Patrick and Siobhan relationship and their subsequent marriage. Patrick was out on a limb as far as his family were concerned.

Being estranged from Aunts and Uncles doesn't mean that you don't know what they participate in and following one sectarian atrocity, Patrick could hold his tongue no more and went to offer information to the Authorities.

The British presence in Northern Ireland met his information gladly and the intelligence network saw in him the opportunity to have an insider in the UDA movement, and he was persuaded, with money inducements of course, to return to the fringe of his family and become an intelligence asset in the Protestant organisation.

It is possible to continue that double life with a great deal of luck and as he was already the black sheep of the family, with a Catholic wife, his double existence became even more tense.

So, it was that a piece of information too close to home had him targeted by the UVF, the even more violent arm of the protestant organisation, had the British Army spirit them out very quickly for their own safety.

The witness protection programme gave them new identities, new professions, and new surroundings in which to live, but that had to be in Britain. In a matter of 20 years, they had moved four times and only the last position in Bristol had given them any sense of security.

Patrick had a love affair with motorcycles, so it was quite easy for him to accept the position that was offered within a franchise for Yamaha in Bristol. He was remarkably successful in that role and was able to salt away sufficient funds to buy out the company himself.

Unfortunately, his success was his undoing because the raised profile that he acquired increased the liability of him being identified by those who chose revenge for his past betrayal.

The move to Wyrevale was thus brought about after the seeking of yet another move for safety. Patrick was to retain his only connection with Yamaha through the Viceroy motorcycle that was his proud possession, and alongside Jez with his Harley Davidson; the pair had become riding buddies.

The stresses and strains of constant movement and the daily worry of being discovered had a serious effect on Siobhan's mental state, which she managed by turning to alcohol.

She was known by all to be a serious drinker, although that wasn't apparent on a day-to-day basis, any social occasion going would see her drunk. It was a regular occurrence for Siobhan to consume three bottles of wine at dinner much of which she did not eat but would pass around the table. The drink was enough.

Already a very talkative individual, the wine would make her louder and more repetitive and she would want to dominate any conversation that might be occurring amongst the table guests. Almost as though she needed the reassurance of the attention it brought to bolster psyche against the angst in her life.

Siobhan and Patrick lived on Devils Rise, a house purchased for them by the British Government, and Patrick's new work mode was with a small engineering company based on the outskirts of Northwich, making parts for the Salt Mining industry. Subsidised heavily by the Government, that company was never going to fail. Patrick therefore had an easy part to play as the chief engineer.

Siobhan did not work, the allowance paid to them supported her stay-at-home lifestyle, where she spent most of her time either watching rubbish TV or buying and selling jewellery on the internet.

It was a hobby not a job, but kept her in pocket money, sufficient to fund the alcohol addiction. Siobhan, of course, did not acknowledge that she was an alcoholic, but talked more about being a person who enjoyed life in and around a bottle of Sauvignon Blanc.

Many of the residents had a love hate relationship with Siobhan because she was a very generous individual and would do anything to help someone, yet when she drank, she was a serious liability and could be extremely embarrassing if dining in a restaurant.

Siobhan had many acquaintances on the Park but few true friends. The nearest person to her was Claire whom she had supported closely following the sudden death of her

Father, giving good counsel whilst dispensing wine to drown the sorrows.

CHAPTER EIGHT

Claire and Richard

Claire was a seriously wealthy individual and apart from George and Amy, her husband Richard and she were the richest residents in Wyrevale. They owned one of the bespoke houses on the Views next door to George and Amy, on which they had no mortgage.

Claire was the only child in her family and her mother had died quite early when Claire was only thirteen. Quite understandably, she became remarkably close to her father. Bryan owned a chain of DIY stores throughout Cheshire, Lancashire and North Wales and was made a multi-millionaire by the sale of these to a national organisation for £80 million pounds.

At age 60, Bryan with all his wealth behind him decided that he would pursue adventure holidays and travel the world; something he had not been able to do whilst building his company. He ventured to New Zealand to do the highest bungee jump and white-water rafting. To Africa to climb Mount Kilimanjaro and go sky diving over the Grand Canyon in Arizona. He enjoyed every minute of it and every minute he was away troubled Claire.

His last trip was to sail the Atlantic in the annual yacht race from Las Palmas in the Canary Islands to St. Lucia in the Caribbean. The ARC (Atlantic Race for Cruisers) was an annual event for sailing cruisers of which Bryan had some experience in his younger days, sailing out of Conwy in North Wales.

Sailing in the Menai Straits and out into the Irish Sea can present its problems of tide and weather, but nothing in comparison to the seas that can be experienced once crossing the Atlantic.

Bryan had booked himself on as a crew member on a 50ft Oyster yacht. A trip of that nature can take up to 17 days Island to Island depending on the type of yacht used and the experience of the crew on board.

For Bryan, the trip was to last only 7 days as a storm broke 7 days into their crossing when Bryan was at the helm during a night-time watch. Calling all the crew on board to reef the sails and lower the jib, Bryan was at his busiest, too busy to secure himself and was lost overboard.

Being dark and in mountainous seas, he was soon lost from sight of the only crew member who saw him fall. The boat was turned back and spent several hours until daylight looking for Bryan, but they were unable to find him, not even a body.

His loss was radioed to Race organisers in Las Palmas, and they had the challenging task of relaying the information back to his only living relative, Claire.

Claire was to inherit her father's fortune which, after death duties amounted to in excess of £45 million. Such a considerable sum, however, could not replace a father on whom she doted, and his death was to have a long-lasting effect on her disposition and attitude to life.

She began not eating properly and became obsessed with physical fitness and at 6ft tall the dramatic weight loss was clear for all to see. Many friends and neighbours would offer their support and in that respect Siobhan, who went along with Claire's gym obsession was the closest. Whilst Claire lost weight and became anorexic, Siobhan's drinking maintained her weight at 12 stone which given her stature at 5ft 9in did not look too obvious.

Claire's husband of 12 years, Richard had met her through his connection with her father's company, to whom he supplied hardware, locks, hinges screws etc that he manufactured in his own company.

Claire's Father had invited Richard to a company golf day where Claire was acting as hostess when she was twenty-four, Richard was thirty. From there their relationship grew and she married at age 28.

Her Father was lost at sea in the week of her 30th birthday and expecting her first child but Richard was there in support.

From then on, he did not seem to notice the downward spiral towards the anorexic state, praising her for her trim figure.

Richard and Claire were to have three children which they managed despite her malnourished condition. Toby was the oldest to be followed by twin girls, Polly, and Isobel. Now at age 40 with the children aged 10 and 8 her life revolved around them and her daily keep fit obsession.

Husband Richard seemed oblivious to the damage she was reeking upon herself and openly stated how he admired her slim, trim figure.

Even at the Summer Ball, a black-tie event, it was clear that Claire was playing with her food. Admittedly that evening's menu was not Haute Cuisine, with a serving of Tomato and Basil Soup, Chicken stuffed with mushrooms and pancetta and seasonal vegetables, followed by a desert choice of vanilla/chocolate cheesecake or lemon tart.

Claire had two spoonsful of soup, gave Richard the Chicken, and ate a portion of vegetables, declining on the desert. Many people wanted to say how they thought she was too thin, but it was difficult to finding an opening to do that.

Claire would continue in her way without being aware of the dangers to her well-being, and totally unaware of the concern others had for her; not least amongst those was Nikki whose nursing background new the signs all too clearly.

CHAPTER NINE

Nikki was nineteen

Born on the Commonwealth of Dominica, Nikki was nineteen when she commenced her nurse training course at Ross University in Portsmouth on the Northern tip of the Island.

Nikki's parents, like many of the older inhabitants of Dominica had not had the benefit of secondary education and when their daughter succeeded in gaining a common entrance exam place at the high school in Roseau, they were overjoyed.

Following her career through secondary school, they were keen that she develop a worthwhile future position and saw in nursing, a dedicated profession, which fitted well with Nikki's specialist subjects. Nikki was therefore encouraged to seek a place to train as a nurse. Nikki was nineteen.

It was the year that Roger had been accepted from his position in Antigua to further his medical studies, and by that time had been a single man for several years. Roger would be present at Ross for three years and during that time would attend many of the student social functions.

It was in his second year that he first made contact with a nursing student in her second year of studies.

There was an instant mutual attraction, but neither of the parties would acknowledge that publicly for several months. but by the end of that second year, Roger who was a long time out of the dating habit, plucked up enough courage to ask Nikki out to dinner. She did not refuse.

Both of them were to qualify at the University and Nikki would start a permanent position in the hospital.

Roger with his micro-biological background had acquired is medical degree, on a fast track a year earlier, was a prime candidate for a junior registrar position in the pathology department which he would have been accepted gratefully, but he wished to further his studies in Chicago.

He obtained resident status very quickly and could have continued his life there. However, he had not forgot the nurse in Dominica and set about his return to the Island.

Three years later at the age of fifty he was to head up the Pathology department at Ross and realise that the love of his life was ever present on the hospital nursing staff.

His proposal was readily accepted by Nikki who had been harbouring the desire for all of those years since they first met and dated.

Nikki was now thirty-one.

Nikki's parents were highly delighted, for now not only had their daughter obtained an exceptionally good education, a professional career and good standing in the community, but now she was to marry a doctor and professor to boot.

The extended family however were not that keen on that union and were unhappy with mixed race marriages.

They were to marry in April 1995 in the local Baptist Church on the outskirts of Roseau which overlooked the Cruise Liner dock. The Church was where her family had attended faithfully all her life.

The reception was held in the Hotel which dominates the Roseau skyline, Fort Young. A former military outpost, the Hotel had a superb terrace overlooking the Caribbean Sea.

With the sun setting out west on the horizon and the waves gently lapping on the shore below, the setting was idyllic.

Roger had managed to invite his two children over for the wedding and they had arrived at the local airport via a LIAT flight from Barbados where their Virgin Atlantic flight from London Gatwick had landed on the previous day.

Dominic, now in his late thirties was to function as Roger's best man and Nikki had Samantha as a bridesmaid.

The happy couple were to spend the first night of their honeymoon in the Scots Head suite at Fort Young. A large attractively furnished three room apartment, had a separate balcony opening out to a view across the Caribbean Sea to the Scots Head peninsula on the southern tip of the Island.

They enjoyed their life together in Dominica with its tropical rainforests and some say a river for every day of the year, unlike Antigua who claimed to have a beach for every day of the year.

Roger's medical research led him to accumulate many patented remedies from which he was to receive many royalties over the coming years. These were aimed at those tropical diseases for which the Antiguan Government had originally employed him.

On his retirement at 60, Roger had decided that now that Nikki's parents were deceased, he would ask her to move back to the UK. That decision coincided with an offer from a large drug company in the United States for one of his patents. The offer was sufficiently large that he could not refuse, setting them both up financially for the rest of their lives.

Seeking a new life in the UK, they had to choose a place to live. The drive behind that would be to choose a place close enough to his children, so that should grandchildren arrive they could be seen on a regular basis.

Both Dominic and Samantha lived in the North of England, Dominic in Altrincham, and Samantha in Wilmslow, both suburbs south of Manchester.

Seeking luxury, they stumbled upon a brochure for a new development in the Cheshire countryside, Wyrevale, that conveniently, was about twenty miles from both of the children.

Attracted by the housing alongside water features, they were one of the first couples to purchase a property in the Brookdale site on their release.

Being just the two of them, they considered that these houses, the smaller of the properties on the development, were sufficiently large enough for them and would have enough bedrooms to accommodate guests and potential grand children at any time.

Considered small the house was to have six bedrooms, four bathrooms and three reception rooms over three floors. Being the first to purchase they were able to select the prime location being bordered by the brook at the rear and overlooking the fifth hole on the golf course.

As early tenants of Wyrevale, Nikki and Roger were in the vanguard of the Residents Association and through that quickly developed a circle of friends which had held together for more than 10 years. The group, in its infancy, would have a membership of around thirty but as the years rolled on, closer relationships would blossom with the circle now comprised of the attendees at the summer ball.

As the group reduced in size, other members who were there at the beginning would drift off to become nodding acquaintances who would periodically meet at social events. The Golf Club influence could be seen by the respective cliques which grew.

On the next table to the one that George had booked and onto which Roger and Nikki had been invited were Derek and Michelle, James and Paula, Frankie, and Sabina and her husband Graham. Frankie did not have a regular escort but would turn up with one of her current four men in tow.

A third table saw the remaining group of residents who would attend any charity event to be seen. There would be Michael and Suzanne, Colin, Dina, Tony, and Maria. The connections here were truly through the female members except that Maria would be there with Tony as a mark of respectability, as everyone knew that Tony's extra-marital affairs were very current, and that Susie was the real desire.

As Roger had retired with sufficient wealth Nikki was able to enjoy life without working and had engaged a bucket list of Trophy places which she had visited or which she wanted to visit in the coming years.

Roger who had enjoyed the prospect of doing absolutely nothing in his retirement save his hobby interest in photography, was happy to haul his camera equipment around the chosen venues.

As a couple they had a particular liking for Italy, and spent many a long weekend in Florence, Rome or Venice and holiday weeks on Capri. In later life these would only be a memory.

CHAPTER TEN

Tony

Tony was fifty-six.

An ex-marine commando and one-time member of the SAS he stood 6ft 2in tall and still carried the muscular figure that was necessary for the role he played in the military.

In the latter years of his army career, he was responsible for the supply and maintenance of the uniquely specialised vehicles that his type of warfare required, the high-speed boats, the converted Land Rovers, and the desert vehicles much akin to beach buggies.

On his discharge it was not unusual therefore, that he should continue using all the knowledge gained whist in the service.

He created his own engineering company, Millparts, which specialised in the construction of specialised vehicles and the supply of replacement parts not only to the military establishment but also to the auto industry.

One of the first people to realise the value of 3D printing, his company expanded incredibly early into that aspect of engineering, gaining contracts to supply bespoke parts and components.

Building on the special vehicle interests, he was approached by the film industry to construct replica machines which were to star in many action movies.

The ability to produce these bespoke parts led him to supply several of the then current Formula One racing teams, in their quest for greater aerodynamic efficiency, with wind tunnel models made directly from the digital images of the design team.

The military contracts alone had made Tony a wealthy man, and the diversity that 3D printing brought only added to his wealth and prestige. Tony was a workaholic, and the success of his company was down to the long hours he put in personally. That however was to the detriment of his personal life and his relationships suffered badly once the company was up and running.

Whilst in the Army, Tony had married Bridget and their marriage survived the many overseas tours and the uncertainty of return that that involved. Bridget remained at home and brought up two children, both boys. With the initial success of Tony's company, they had bought a house in Devil's Rise and could be seen occasionally in the Golf Club bar.

Tony would be more visible, as when the sun was shining, he would bring out his prized E-Type Jaguar, driving off into the North Wales countryside purely for the pleasure that can only be experienced by those individuals whose hearts are fuelled by high octane engines and wind in the hair excitement.

Bridget was not a fan of the E-type, as driving an open top sports car with wind in your hair did nothing for expensively coiffured hair style. Tony would always want the roof off and was a strong enough character to make that happen.

With his workaholic nature, Tony was rarely at home. With the diversification into the film industry, making model 3D sets for CGI enhancement of blockbuster films; his attachment to the Formula One scene, his business contracts necessitated long absences from home to ensure those contracts were maintained, and to push the company even further forward.

Although Bridget had survived the Army adventures, these prolonged periods alone resulted in her turning to the Cabernet Sauvignon for comfort.

Wine would help her small depressions, but when the consumption occurs on a daily basis, at a level approaching a bottle a day and more at weekends, her body succumbed to alcoholism.

No one would be aware of that, as it was generally confined to the home, until one fateful day when on leaving the development in her Audi Q7 she managed to demolish a row of trees that lined the exit road near the security lodge.

Fortunately, she was not severely hurt, and the security personal were rapidly on hand to help her away from the wreckage and assist with the ambulance crew. The story and the damage were there for all to see as they passed the security barriers each day.

Tony was not prepared to accept her behaviour anymore and had already begun an extra-marital affair long before the accident and the move away from his relationship with Bridget was made simpler as he had Maria on the scene.

His wealth was such that Tony was able to allow Bridget to remain in the marital home with the children, who were now in their teenage years, and purchase an apartment in the Old Abbey. Maria moved in shortly afterwards as they had been together now for more than eight years.

Maria was not the first affair Tony had had, for shortly after setting up the company, he employed an extremely attractive PA in Pat. His troubled marriage was his excuse to justify the extension of their business association into a full-blown affair.

It was said that that was one of the contributing factors that turned Bridget to the Cabernet, and its development beyond a social drink. She was fully aware of Tony's inability to keep it in his trousers.

Tony had agreed to remove Pat from the business in an attempt to placate Bridget and reduce her alcohol consumption, but his wandering eye and hands were soon to find Maria and following the Q7 road accident he gave up Bridget completely.

Maria had moved into the apartment with Tony about five years before the Summer Ball and had become a close friend of Joan, Alex's wife. She was known to help Joan with her internet business, for her own background had been in business administration. Tony and Maria would appear happy at these social functions, but with a five-year history to their relationship, Tony was restless again.

The gossip in the Park was that Tony had been seen with another woman. Nikki had seen him in the local town hand in hand with a blonde-haired woman who was not Maria but had a remarkably close resemblance to her. They did not try to hide their closeness and although Nikki was in the same shop, they chose not to acknowledge her.

Obviously, that small bit of information was soon being passed round the local ladies' forum and so everyone at the summer ball except Maria, knew that once again Tony was spreading it around.

Derek and Michelle were neighbours of Tony when he was with Bridget, so they had a keen interest in discovering as much as possible about the new affair.

Bridget still lived next door, as Tony had left her in residence when he bought the apartment, and it was from Bridget that Michelle discovered that the new lady was called Susie.

Shortly after the Summer Ball, Tony quit the apartment, leaving Maria to settle all his bills, and moved off the Park.

The vacancy left behind once he had departed, gave Maria a boost in the community for there were many who felt that she had been badly treated. That position was reinforced when one-day Maria confessed to Michelle that she had frequently been subjected to violent physical abuse by Tony and on many occasions, had declined invitations because of the bruising.

Tony in his way had been very clever in only hitting in those areas normally covered by clothing but Maria new they were there and was too embarrassed to be seen in public.

Her continued existence with Tony during these events was common to all battered wives who are reluctant to move away and continue to receive the abuse.

Maria was able to keep the Abbey apartment and would begin to develop her own life without him, developing her own business in interior design, and would continue to be one of the Ladies who lunched

CHAPTER ELEVEN

Derek and Michelle

Derek and Michelle were an odd couple. Derek was 5-foot 9in tall, shaven headed and carrying a substantial beer belly. He was a true salesman and would talk the hind legs off a donkey given half the chance.

He was a golf partner of Jez and regularly made up a weekend four with Michael and James.

He was known for his loud golf attire and even Ian Poulter would struggle to match the outlandish nature of his colour schemes. It is true however that Poulter would have a greater degree of style, as Derek's combinations had to be seen to be believed.

Blue and white check trousers, orange polo shirt and green golf shoes topped off with a black pork pie hat. The golf bag, of course, had to come in bright two tones as well.

Michelle, by contrast, was six feet tall with deep auburn hair which fell below her waistline when not immaculately styled on top. Her dress sense was impeccable, and she would never be seen without presenting an elegant appearance. She had developed that style from an early modelling career and carried that forward into her own retail outlet successfully selling designer fashions in the local town.

Both Derek and Michelle had been married before. Michelle in her modelling days had fallen head over heels for a young photographer who had been there at the beginning of her career. He was responsible for lifting her from an early beauty contest to the modelling environment. They were married for two years.

It was a marriage doomed to fail, as the temptation to the photographer of all the young nubile women he was to photograph, was far too great for fidelity. Michelle called it a day when she returned back late to the studio to find her husband deeply engrossed in his work, but much more intimately than she was prepared to tolerate.

As the marriage failed, Michelle gave up modelling and suffered several years of acute depression thinking she had lost her attractiveness and was no longer a desirable female.

Derek had started his working life straight from university with his marketing degree. He had sought various positions in the marketing departments of large companies and was finally taken on by the Mars Corporation in their Pedigree Pet Food Company. He was to follow that with four other positions each lasting a mere couple of years.

Derek's work ethic was based on putting in awfully long hours, but what he did not realise was that the hours he spent could well have been much shorter had he learnt the art of time management. All too eager to talk and not work, his daily routine would only be completed once everyone in the office had left and there was no one left to talk to.

He was under the mistaken belief that these long hours were impressive to the management above, but whenever a depression in the particular sector he was working in came along, he was the first to be let go, hence the numerous positions in so few years.

His first wife was Naomi, who soon realised that his long absences could not be tolerated and sought a divorce and new life after four years.

The two of them, Derek and Michelle were therefore single again and in their early thirties. Each decided that not only a new life was needed but a new location too. Derek moved from Derby and Michelle from Blackpool to seek these new horizons in Manchester.

When you are single at 31, your need to seek new connections can be a tiresome business. It is however much easier these days with advent of the internet and web sites such as Match.com to research the available market.

Back in the 1980's the internet did not give you that opportunity, but there were dating companies around, Dateline for an example. That company would regularly advertise their services in the Sunday papers, and it was on one early Sunday morning in January that Derek plucked up the courage to complete the psychological profile questionnaire and post it off to Dateline.

Coincidentally Michelle was to follow the same pathway.

The system employed by Dateline was to match profiles and send the applicant a list of six names and telephone numbers, where upon the recipient was encouraged to call. No pictures available and no video profile available; just six numbers.

Cold calling is a difficult entity in its own right, but to call in the belief that the telephone will be answered by an individual with whom you may want to date, required a leap of faith.

Derek received his list within a week of his application but would not develop enough confidence for a further two weeks to pick up the handset and dial.

Had he not had a New Year where his depression had meant that he spent the four-day holiday without leaving his bed, he would not have been in that position, but that near suicidal weekend had grown a positive desire to rectify his personal relationships.

Michelle had been in her depressed period for more than 2 years, and the arrival of her six names was her attempt to grow out of that. She too took more than 3 weeks to attempt her first call.

Derek had received his list on a Friday, so it seemed appropriate to commence his quest on a weekend. The application form allowed the applicant to specify a radius of distance in which the search for a partner should be contained. Derek had set that at 30 miles from his residence in Didsbury, South Manchester. The phone numbers he received varied beyond the ubiquitous 0161 Manchester regional code.

The first number on the list was not a 0161 code, and he did not recognise the area in which the potential date lived. Plucking up the courage to dial, a woman's voice answered but it was clear that that was a much older lady than that on the list; she turned out to be the mother of the applicant.

Whether she knew that her daughter had made that sortie into dating was not clear but trying to explain why he was calling her daughter was extremely embarrassing, and she was not helpful. Apparently, her daughter, Theresa was washing her hair. Derek left his number, but no return call was received.

The second and third numbers returned no answer and Derek was becoming dispirited but vowed to complete the six. The final three numbers were a challenge.

Number four was the first to be successful; the girl on the end of the line was interested in a meet and agreed to meet that day, but as she couldn't drive, she asked Derek to call at her house to collect her. So, at eight o'clock on the Saturday night, Derek presented himself on the doorstep of a small cottage in Cheadle Hulme. Jackie, the lady in question opened the door at first knock.

It is a horrible sensation when your first thoughts are

 "Please let us go somewhere where no one knows me,"

as the physical appearance of Jackie was not one to which Derek would normally be attracted.

However, they departed to the Church Inn on the Bramall Road where their evening, initially quite stilted turned out to be more pleasant than he had imagined at first sight.

Jackie was a librarian and had all the qualities of the stereotypical character of the profession. Her manner and conversation were however not unpleasant. The evening finished early with Derek taking her home at 11 and although invited in for coffee, could not wait to leave as soon as possible. As that was the first attempt, no follow up occurred.

The evening could well have put Derek off, but he was determined to see it through. Waking on the Sunday morning he tried number 5 on the list. That one, Pauline, was again anxious to meet as soon as possible and a time was set for 7.30 that same day. Pauline too could not drive so at 7.30 Derek was pulling up outside 86 Victoria Road, in Stretford.

On opening the door, Pauline did a twirl in the manner of the then popular Generation Game with Bruce Forsyth and Isla. A large lady, the twirl was meant to impress because once invited into the house, Derek was given the opportunity to walk away if he did not like what her saw. Having made the commitment to the evening, he was reluctant to walk as he saw that as very insulting to a person whom he did not know and who might be much more than her outward appearance.

Pauline was a Domestic Science teacher at the secondary school in Stretford and the furnishings, cushions and curtains were all of her own design and construction. She did indeed show talent in that field. As for the evening before, they set off for a local pub, arriving at a large Victorian gin palace at the end of Upper Chorlton Road.

Conversation was much easier with Pauline, and although Derek was not usually attracted to the larger ladies, there was something about Pauline that made the evening fly by. Taking Pauline home, Derek was again invited in for coffee and the conversation continued beyond midnight, progressing to the odd kiss.

Whether it was attraction or the fact that both parties were sexually starved, the kissing became more intense and quickly developed into much more than an odd peck on the cheek. Derek was invited to stay for the night, and his acute arousal could not say no. The night was to proceed with four episodes of intercourse and little sleep.

Derek had to be in his office at 9 am the following day so had to make an exit at around 5am to get home, have an hour's sleep, shower, change and arrive on time with has much energy as possible. The evening had left its mark on Derek, but he was not to see Pauline again despite her several attempts to contact him. The events of that night lay heavy on Derek and whether it was guilt or shame that drove him away he did not want a repeat, even though the sex had been very enjoyable. When you are hungry you can easily binge and feel guilty afterwards.

Michelle had gone through a similar process to Derek and her list of numbers had Derek on them, and it was she who initiated the contact. Her previous attempts at contact had been blighted by an acute attack of sinusitis which had laid her low for more than two weeks. On the day she approached Derek, she found him laid low with a bad back so was yet again stopped in her quest.

Derek had not given up, so when his bad back was better, he called Michelle back and arranged a rendezvous. Derek arrived early at the Didsbury pub, the chosen venue, and was settling down with his pint of Guinness when in walked that Auburn-Haired tall model like figure. There was an instant physical attraction, and the night was very agreeable, parting with a peck on the cheek. A second date was arranged one week later, and it was only a few days later that they were enjoying each other's company in many ways, not least the wonderful sex that had commenced on their third date on the floor of Derek's apartment.

Now fifteen years on they were the couple who were envied by many on the development. It was clear that Michelle had her fashion business, but it was unclear as to what Derek did or had done in the past to achieve their current financial success.

It was said that a small company he founded in Stockport in the beginning of the mobile phone boom had traded illegally, dodging the tax man with a VAT scam, in so doing he had piled away a considerable sum. It was also said that Derek had reacted quickly to a high-profile legal case which saw two individuals jailed in Holland for such practices. Derek was able to unload his business to a large corporate buyer for the sum of £8 million and was now sitting on that in the bank.

The outward appearance of Derek is that he did extraordinarily little yet was sufficiently funded to have a nice lifestyle and as they had agreed between them, Derek and Michelle had no children. No straightforward evidence was available to substantiate the rumours, but it was noticeably clear that Derek had a large fund behind him.

Michelle liked the good life. She would often be seen attending charity events with a group of girlfriends and was a regular attendee at Chester race Days. The fixture list happened to follow quite quickly after the summer ball, and she had asked Frankie and Sabrina to join her.

Ladies Day in Chester is an excuse to consume substantial amounts of alcohol, and the Group who had no particular interest in Horse Racing were there to drink and be seen. If you aspire to the elevated levels of Society, then you will need to be in the right places at the right time so that the kudos is achieved. In reality of course, the posturing can so easily be derided.

The minibus arrived at 7 in the evening to ferry them back to Wyrevale and it was unfortunate for these ladies who wished lofty ideals to vomit all over the back of the driver's seat whilst passing along the A556. Michelle would never be able to live that down.

CHAPTER TWELVE

Frankie

Frankie did not live on the Wyrevale development. She had been a resident of the Lakes before her ex-husband decided that sex with the lady golf pro was much better than he was getting at home. The divorce had happened five years earlier when Frankie was thirty-six. Now at 41 she had joined that group of divorced women who the tabloid press had dubbed naughty forties.

These ladies found that their new-found freedom gave them a right to a party lifestyle and quite often the party in question was from a much younger age group. Their sexual maturity was a major attraction to these younger gentlemen, or boys, they were never fussy, and the sex games could be very adventurous.

Frankie currently had four men in tow that she would rotate through the week and never looked better on it. Current favourite was Martin who was thirty-five and had his own company providing storage units in Birmingham. He had sufficient money to run a Jaguar XJ in pale blue with magnolia leather. That car could frequently be seen parked in Frankie's drive and everyone knew that Frankie would not be available for the weekend.

Over the last two years, the number of different vehicles that had parked on that drive would exceed five, but it was a credit to Frankie that the quality was never less than an Audi or Mercedes. Frankie would venture out when she felt she needed new adventures, to the wine bars of nearby Knutsford or Alderley Edge. There she would be seen to be available and many a one-night stand would follow these visits.

Sexually mature and beyond the dangers of pregnancy, the hysterectomy had taken place 7 years before, much of which ex-husband blamed for the lack of marital bliss; now that freedom allowed her to partake of many sexual adventures and the wardrobe contained numerous costumes, Basques, and toys for her amusement. A former gymnast, Frankie had remained very supple throughout her life and the positions she was able to achieve would astonish most of the younger men she would encounter.

Occasionally, like Martin, the liaisons would last a while, but it never seemed to go beyond 3 or 4 months. Maybe that new-found freedom was such an adrenaline rush that a stable lifestyle became boring very quickly. Nights out with the girls of Wyrevale would allow tales of recent conquests, but there was always an underlying suspicion that she had yet to find Mr Right, a quest for whom she denied. Many, if not all, the girls envied the life that seemed so much fun but in reality, it was one of desperation and extreme loneliness.

It is far too easy to assume that the regular party style evenings were ones to be cherished, but if you are truly looking for Mr. Right, and the number of men who passed through who were not, the search seems endless and depressing.

All too soon, the prescriptions of anti-depressants would follow, and the high octane mix with alcohol would only make things worse and bleaker still. Far too many mornings would follow nights where there was no recollection of events and in some one who was much younger, would be labelled reckless.

It is inevitable at Frankie's age, that when Mr Right is found, he will have baggage, and a history that has to be accommodated if the relationship is to work; ex-wife or wives, children ranging from early years to teenage monsters, or married children with grandchildren. It can be a much bumpier ride than the initial meetings would indicate. An ex-wife who has not bothered for years will suddenly realise that the ex-husband is having fun again; fun which she may not be experiencing herself. Suddenly, financial needs become apparent to support ex-families and commitments long put on the back burner. The stresses and strains of such demands never bode well for a happy relationship.

Frankie was to experience that in spades when Steve, the latest in line, looked like a keeper. She had brought him to many of the social occasions which occur on Wyrevale via the Golf Club, formal events, and parties at resident's houses. Suddenly, he was no more, and investigation showed that the wife was not ex-wife and the nights with Frankie were there purely for the sexual gratification that he had been receiving. Frankie was good at that. Variety is the spice of life, so they say, and with her abilities to pose and position it was such an attraction to the men she met, Steve amongst them.

Once again rejected, the trail lost, the pursuit of happiness would begin again. A lunch with her close friend, Michelle, would need to be arranged to unburden herself and maybe lighten the load. Michelle had the background that Frankie wished to use, for her relationship with Derek had developed from a dating experience.

Michelle had not had the benefit of internet dating when she met Derick, but she was quick to point Frankie in that direction and agreed to arrange a Match.com evening with the Ladies circle when they could all observe the talent available and give Frankie advice.

One week later five members of the group, Megan, Claire, Siobhan, Michelle, and Maria arrived sufficiently armed with Prosecco for the dating night experience. All in their own way had experience in failed relationships which they thought qualified them to bring advice to the evening. Video profiles were brought up on the internet, viewed and points awarded. At the end of the evening point scores were added and recommendations made. A thoroughly enjoyable evening was had by all but as to whether it helped Frankie no evidence was forthcoming, and her lonely quest continued.

CHAPTER THIRTEEN

Paula and James.

Paula was married to James. She was tall, very slim, a nice body some would say, with long rustic brown hair. At six feet tall, and taller in heels, she towered over James who stretching to his greatest height could only manage five feet nine. The extra weight he carried around his waistline did nothing to improve his structure.

The waistline was the product of many hours in the car, with frequent motorway meals of not particularly wholesome food. James had been a trouble-shooter for a computer company travelling the roads of the UK to fix problems, although now elevated to his own company; his former travelling existence had remained around his waist.

James's company manufactured cleaning products from a small industrial estate on the outskirts of Sandbach. Formerly the site of the large vehicle manufacturer Foden; the demise of that company and its takeover by the Americans with factory relocation, had vacated large areas of industrial designated land for the development of these small units.

James had been able to establish his company early in the 1990's and it had grown sufficiently for him to come off the road and spend his days behind the large desk, in the large office he had treated himself to. A token he felt that reflected his successful venture.

Despite the outward appearance of that success, James never looked the part. His dress style was poor, mismatched and mis-fitting items; tight fitting shirts barely covering the expansive midline and shoes that only TK Maxx stocked as no one else would by them.

Paula, by contrast, was always immaculately presented as the model figure allowed her to dress that way. It was also part of the OCD from which she suffered giving absolute attention to hygiene and routines to be completed so that nothing bad would happen to her.

Formerly an IT manager for Barclays Bank, Paula had left that position to set up a luxury lingerie shop in nearby Northwich. Her attention to detail was put to the test in the positioning of mannequins, the numbers involved and the opening and closing routines.

At the small warehouse she owned, keys would be introduced into the front door lock. The lock would be opened and closed five times before the door could be opened. Once the alarm was switched off, with a code of 5555, the lights would be illuminated with switches operated five times on and off. Closing times required the reverse procedure.

The stock in the shop was in the upper levels of price. Not the basic Marks and Spencer styles, but much more exotic colours, more lace, less material. Matched sets always appeared on the mannequins in the shop window, and she would arrange for these to be changed every five days, continuing her obsession with that number: five models on the website, five different price ranges and five assorted colours.

James, of course, would have nothing to do with that, and frequently derided her obsessions to anyone who would listen. Not good for the success of a marriage. They had no children, and it would seem that the idea of introducing them into Paula's routines prevented that taking place.

Was it that if she had one child, she would have to have five? Was it the concept of cleanliness, with children not meeting the required standard? No one knew but speculation that they were not the type of people whose right for children, was in the forefront of all who knew them.

In any event, James was now 51 years old and although at 40 Paula was younger; the prospect of lack of harmony was never going to be allowing them to contemplate a family.

One of James's ex-girlfriends was still in the background and on a number of occasions had been seen to arrive at Paula and James's house as part of a group of dinner party guests. The other residents of Wyrevale who knew them would often wonder why such an event would happen. The frequent public arguments of James and Paula would indicate that there was an under swell of disharmony in the marriage which may well have initiated the OCD. Nevertheless, there were times when it was clear that they were in tune with each other and the quest for exotic holidays each year under pinned that observation.

They liked to visit the history of Central America, with the Mayan and Inca people's culture foremost in their holiday agendas. Treks to Machu Picchu would seem to be at odds with the hygiene rules at home, yet it was so part of the togetherness that was there to be seen.

Holidays figured highly on James and Paula's lifeline as they had first met whilst on holiday in Spain. James, who had recently split from his long-term girlfriend after discovering she was having an affair with a long-standing family friend, John a husband of a former school friend, Diane, with whom she had stayed in touch.

Diane married John when they were both 18 years old, and she was pregnant. John was the adventurer in the partnership and felt he had missed out on his youth. Now at 35 John was released from the parenting that had occupied his twenties and sought to find that adventurous spirit from the past. James's ex-girlfriend, Karen, had always found John attractive and given to opportunity to seek some thrills of which she thought were missing in her relationship with James had begun the affair some two years previously.

On breaking up with Karen, James had spent a miserable two years alone but was determined now to take a cheerful outlook to life and had booked a holiday in the Spanish resort of Marbella, staying at the Marbella Beach Club Hotel.

He had a particular fondness of a restaurant there called El Nino and would spend his evenings dining and taking after dinner drinks at the bar. In that year, Paula had come to Marbella with a group of girlfriends. They too were staying at the Hotel which lay just off the main coast road and had taken the walk along the road to dine at El Nino, on the recommendation of the concierge at the hotel. He had said that they would be able to dine on the beach edge, receive gourmet food and wine and experience the glorious view across the bay. It was an experience they could not resist.

After their meal, the girls had retired to the bar to finish their night with a few cocktails, before the short walk back to the Beach Club. Paula had taken a seat next to James who was alone at the bar. As the girls had consumed several bottles of Rioja with their meal and were now on the Cosmopolitans, she was very animated and began a conversation with James. James, immediately attracted to Paula, was all too willing to continue that and before she left had invited her to return the next night for dinner. Paula accepted the invitation. That was the beginning of a whirlwind romance for they were engaged within 3 months and married in 6 months. After their marriage, Paula had given up IT post with Barclays Bank at Radbrooke Hall and formed the online lingerie business which allowed her to work from home.

James and Paula had purchased a home on the Lakes area some two years after their marriage, and although that area of Wyevale was one of the last developments to be completed, they soon established friendships through James's membership of the Golf Club. That association had been the source of many if not all of the friendships that had grown on Wyevale. Over the years however, couples would come and go from their initial associations, and in many cases the long-term attraction of the Golf Club would be left behind with only occasional meetings for drinks or meal occurring.

James however was an avid golfer and set out regularly to lower his handicap and spending a considerable amount of time in the club house after each round. His presence there and his ability to engage fellow members in conversation led very quickly to membership of the golf club committee and a fast-track pathway to the Captaincy of the club. In his 51st year he achieved that position and with it his ego began his decline in friendships around the development.

Paula however had always supported his golf ambitions and initially revelled in being the wife of the captain. The first lady she liked to think of herself. When her local girlfriends began to shy away because of James's developed arrogance, question marks were raised in her mind about the value of such a position. Her close relationship with James who would run their marriage on a tight rein began to loosen and as James was playing the captain to the full and away on many Golf related events, she found herself lonelier than she liked.

Frankie had been a faithful friend and was quick to realise her distress and invited Paula to one of the Wine Bars in Knutsford one week when James was in Turkey on a Golf holiday. Frankie was on the search for company as usual and Paula was to experience that at first hand. She had not been in that environment for more than 15 years and the flirtatious approaches she met were exciting. So much did she enjoy the evening that she asked Frankie to take her again when James was away once more.

On the second visit she was to meet Robert who had been there on their first visit and the evening was much more fun than their previous encounter. Robert had asked her to have coffee with him the following day if she was free. As James was still away and her business was closed on Wednesday afternoons, she agreed to be available at 3pm in the coffee bar he had chosen in Alderley edge as his apartment was there.

She parked her Audi on the station car park and made the short walk across the road with butterflies devouring her insides. Robert was there in the booth at the back on the right. He waved her over and assisted her with her coat whilst she took her seat and ordered a skinny mocha latte. Duly served the two developed their conversation from the night before and it wasn't long before the space between was lost so that they could be much closer together.

Paula had no commitments at home and the invitation to view Robert's apartment was accepted with an anticipation she had not felt for many a year. Approaching forty, but still extremely attractive, she was fascinated that that younger man could be so interesting to her and so thrilling in his attentions. It is not difficult to imagine therefore that the afternoon became an evening and Paula left to open the shop on Thursday with a new life buzz.

James who was on the Costa del Sol playing Golf had been curious to wonder why his calls and text messages had not been answered but was relieved when Paula called from the shop on Thursday. She explained that her battery levels had been low, and she had left the phone on charge the previous day in the shop forgetting to take it home with her. James and Paula, like many tech savvy individuals had no land line at home so the mobile connection was the only one open to James.

On his return from Spain, James was to discover a different Paula; one who had released her OCD inhibitions and one who would not so easily submit to his control. His life had changed, and the tensions were increasing. As his Captain year was still only halfway through, he had to continue his commitment and there were many more opportunities for Paula to meet Robert.

James had his suspicions that there was someone else in Paula's life, a driving force that had changed their relationship. He began to consume much more of the draught Peroni in the golf club before coming home and many nights returned quite intoxicated. That of course fuelled Paula's increasing distaste for James and his golf addiction. James's drinking was to be his downfall.

A golf member had recently acquired a bright red Ferrari and was proudly presenting it to his fellow golfers in the car park at the side of the Abbey and they had retired to the bar. James had been in the bar for more than two hours and was leaving much worse for wear and as the roads in Wyrevale were private had no worry about drink driving. He pulled away from the car park and began the climb uphill to the main park road. His ability to control the Lexus 4 x 4 was reduced and he was able to spread white paint all down the side of that Ferrari but was confident that no one had seen that event and did not stop. It was unfortunate therefore that his private number plate was deposited alongside the Ferrari in the car park.

It is rare that a Captain of a Golf Club is dismissed mid-season, but the Abbey Vale Club committee were not prepared to accept James's apology. His place was taken by the current Vice-Captain. The effect on Paula and James's relationship was traumatic. Paula, although staying in the marital home was determined to live a life outside of the tight rein with which she had been controlled in the eight previous years. To all on the development the change had been foreseen once the Ego Captain had been created.

CHAPTER FOURTEEN

Colin and Dina

Colin and Dina had moved back to Wyrevale when Colin had taken a position at a mid-Cheshire college. He had viewed that as a rundown of his life towards retirement. Dina was not entirely happy with that arrangement, but since her job role covered the whole of the country, a central home base was an advantage.

Dina was in charge of a large, cooled water distribution organisation. Angel Falls was the name of the company, and she drove the company E-class Mercedes convertible, still with the fish symbol. Colin had a Ford Fiesta, maybe the only adult driven one on the development and that was exactly the level of his desired image.

Theirs was not a happy marriage, and despite the outward appearance of all in harmony, the marriage was deeply troubled. Dina had left before, and at Jez's party, Dina was recounting to the ladies how in one month's time she was moving again, leaving Colin behind. The Ford Fiesta had turned to bite him.

The seasons had moved on however, and now at the Golf Club annual Christmas party, Colin and Dina were still together and were forming the fifth couple at George and Amy's table making up the usual ten members invited. The function as was normal was staged in the function room above the bar in the Old Abbey Clubhouse.

Tables of ten set out to accommodate 120 leaving sufficient space for the disco and DJ on the small, elevated platform, could hardly be called a stage, in the left-hand corner next to the door. A small bar was staffed in the opposite corner.

Mass catering is always a gamble and the menu for the evening had rack of lamb as the main course, with the vegetarian option of goat's cheese and spinach tart. When the service is slow, as it was on that evening, the wine will flow and those that were inclined would consume more than others.

George had arranged for six bottles of wine to be placed on the table, red and white mixed, but Dina had insisted that a sparkling wine should be ordered, acquiring three bottles of Prosecco to begin the night.

After waiting an hour, the soup course was served and was a reasonable tomato and basil. The main course that followed however was a disaster and the rack of lamb was practically raw. It is acknowledged that lamb is best served pink, but when the blood runs freely it is not acceptable.

Claire, who was present with Richard, had strange dietary habits as they knew that her meal be returned to the chef. Others followed and soon the table was reduced to consume the wine once more. A second attempt by the kitchen proved no better than the first and all the meals were left uneaten.

It was becoming apparent that Colin and Dina had consumed a substantial proportion of the wine available as their behaviour was to take a bizarre turn.

Everyone knew that the marriage was not good, as Dina had informed the Ladies of the table at Chester Races in the summer, and yet here at a table of ten in the brightly lit function room of the Golf Club were a couple acting as though they were newly met and desperate need of sexual gratification.

Colin had at first put his arm around Dina for a gentle kiss, but Dina had responded with a neck grabbing, deep tongue thrusting response. Colin who, after two bottles of Shiraz, was already florid and hot under the collar was not going to reject that approach.

His hands which were around Dina's neck now moved forward and were gently progressing south, whilst their deep throated embrace continued.

Dina, whose tall long legged blonde figure was the envy of many of the women present, was known for her choice of short cocktail dresses and as she moved across from her seat to Colin's lap, little was left unseen with the view provided by Marks and Spencer.

Once in place she produced an elaborate interpretation of lap dancing to the disco music from Saturday Night fever, whilst the eight remaining members of the table tried to pretend that was not happening.

Dina was a lawyer by profession having come to that late, taking her degree at Keele University when she was thirty-six and before they had moved to East Anglia.

The paucity of jobs in the legal profession had given her the push into management, and whilst Colin was at East Anglia, she was able to obtain her MBA. Her natural tendency towards an eco-friendly lifestyle had given her the opportunity to work with the pure water company, owned by her father, with whom she had made amends from an early split in her life.

The company sourced its water from a spring on her father's large property in the Peak District and the money available to Dina explained how they were able to fund their Brookdale property. Colin's salary at Mid-Cheshire would not have been sufficient.

Colin and Dina's early life was never discussed, but it was speculated that their lifestyle was derived from a beginning fuelled by North American experiences, possibly drug related and certainly obtained from commune groups.

Colin's musical background was a source of wonder, particularly the connection with the Deep South of the USA and the ukulele. Shades of duelling banjos and the 1972 film Deliverance would be appropriate. Dina would have had that hippy lifestyle too.

Commune living is not easily funded, and although Colin had his musical groups that could pick money from the small gigs they managed to attract, their music was not mainstream and did not attract large audiences or venues.

Dina had no particular skills at that stage and had contributed to the funds by presenting herself to a local gentleman's Club where she had become very proficient in the art of lap-dancing. The evening's table demonstrations were obviously a throwback to that era.

In 1995 on one of Colin's trips to the Deep South, Dina had become inspired by the heavily influenced Baptist society, joining one of the many evangelical communities that abound within that geography.

Many of the Baptist ministers are great orators and can easily persuade any of a mind that the lifestyle they profess, is the way forward, despite the scandalous behaviour of some of their colleagues regularly reported in the media. Dina, whose life with Colin had always been one of difficulties, had at that time being going through a deep depression, and in the enlightenment given to her by the Reverend Truman Mitchell found Jesus. Her born again Christianity would stay with her for her life to come.

The behaviour on the night of the Christmas party was in complete contrast to the perceived devout Christian and was taken by all at the table as one which would confirm many of the suspected but not proven tales that followed Colin and Dina around.

The biggest of all was that Dina had in fact been a lap dancer at one time, and it was Roger the consummate listener who had picked that in conversation one social event whilst sitting next to Dina in her cups.

Their conversation had evolved from the intake of alcohol, Roger was almost teetotal, to drug use. Dina had confessed to using everything in her time but had never injected heroin. It was the enlightenment that had steered her away from that lifestyle. The drug habit had been paid for by the part time job in the gentleman's clubs, unspecified.

It would only be four weeks before Colin and Dina were living apart again, with Colin remaining in the house in Brookdale and Dina taking an apartment in the Abbey. So apart but separated only by the one-mile circuit of the peripheral road. It would appear that that was a convenience that allowed both to appear as couple at future social events.

'Nowt as funny as folk'

as they say.

CHAPTER FIFTEEN

Party animals

Ever the party animals, Jez and Megan would always have an open house on Christmas Day morning, and all were invited to come along whenever their family commitments allowed, as long as it was before 12. Megan would lay on canapés and nibbles with plenty of alcohol for consumption.

Following the events of the Golf Club Christmas Party the main topic of conversation revolved around the behaviour of Colin and Dina, and as they rarely appeared at Jez and Megan's on Christmas Day all were free to air their views on the witnessed performance.

There were mixed expressions of surprise which emanated from two sources.

Firstly, the outward expression of moral reform that had taken over Dina's life since her conversion by the Deep South Baptist Minister, which she would demonstrate on a day-to-day basis and secondly the conclusion that she must have been a successful lap dancer in her time.

These views were split along gender lines, where the women present held on to

"How could she do that when she has the deeply confirmed moral values"

and the men taking on

"We knew those long legs had been developed for purposes other than walking to church each week."

That tongue in cheek view obviously did not go down to well with wives' present.

As always at these gatherings the ladies would consume a considerable number of bottles of their tipple of the moment, Prosecco.

Like the market in general that Italian wine had supplanted champagne as the drink of the chattering classes and at a considerably cheaper price. Discount supermarkets were selling gallons of the wine and at a reasonable price too. Pushed on by favourable critical examinations the wine was considered to be excellently drinkable.

Once you have consumed the contents of a bottle then the effects become noticeable, louder conversations, louder laughs and occasionally but fortunately rarely, angry attitudes.

That year one such event saw Siobhan come to terms with Paula over the small but delicate problem of cats, for Paula was a devoted cat lover.

Siobhan hated cats. T

The dispute arose because Paula's black cat, Rupert, only Paula could call a cat Rupert, had been using Siobhan's garden as a regular toilet stop, she alleged, much to her dismay. Having twice in the last week entered her house complete with cat excrement on her shoes; she was none too keen on the pet to whom Paula was defending.

Paula of course took the stance that if Siobhan did less drinking and spent more time in making sure her garden was tidy, and then she would not have had the misfortune to collect the cat crap on her shoes.

Siobhan, known to consume several bottles a week, had on that morning downed at least two and her Irishness was coming increasingly to the fore, along with a very quick temper.

The Irish are known for their liberal use of four-letter words and Siobhan was not holding back. Jez could only tolerate so much of that and intervened to ask Patrick to take Siobhan home.

Patrick took umbrage to that too and it was with extreme difficulty and a considerable amount of diplomacy that Jez managed to get the two of them through the door.

Paula, who had appeared together with James for the first time in many months, felt obliged to leave too, giving the remaining members, more fuel to the gossip about their relationship, one that had already been circulating when the Colin and Dina episode had happened at the Golf Club Party.

James followed like a dog with its tail between its legs. Which side of the debate that you took depended entirely on your like or dislike of cats, or your considered view on the amount of wine that Siobhan could consume in such a small space of time?

James had only been tolerated once more following his unfortunate driving incident because Megan had kept in close contact with Paula during the troubles.

As Siobhan and Patrick lived on Devils Rise and James and Paula occupied a house alongside the Lakes it seemed impossible that the black cat that Siobhan had seen in her garden could have come from a residence more than one mile away, but she was adamant that the felon was definitely Rupert.

It is possible of course to imagine that a cat on a nightly hunting expedition could have ventured that far to explore the woodland that lay in and around the houses on Devils rise, for they had been designed specifically to blend in with the rising wooded hillside above the Abbey from where the spring water rose to source the brook that ran through Brookdale. A plentiful supply of small rodents would occupy those woods.

The brook had been the original source of power in the monasterial days of the Abbey and would have been powerful enough in its day to drive the mill wheels that fed the monks.

Dina's company had enquired about use of the source water for her drinking water company but had been met by serious objections from residents, particularly those in Brookdale who enjoyed the babbling brook around their lower cost houses, giving them extra kudos in the retail housing market.

The campaign leader in that respect had been Roger whose environmental background had allowed him to make a genuine case. Roger's friendship with the more affluent members of Wyrevale, particularly George had given him the legal back up to defeat the planning application.

Roger and Nikki had never been that friendly with Colin and Dina for Nikki's Caribbean religious background could not accept that Dina's Baptist conversion was sincerely held when she could put on a display such as that at the Golf Club. Nikki believed that Dina had only taken to the role of devout Christian to regain access to levels of Society from whom she had originally descended into the hippy commune life in her early twenties.

It was clear to see that although the many members of that social group appeared to be connected there were clear lines of demarcation that had steadily grown over the fifteen years that the development had grown. Early settlers considered themselves to be pioneers and late comers to be somewhat akin to interlopers.

Once the party had begun to break up, Jez and Megan were left with the daunting task of clearing the dishes and it being Christmas too. George, Amy, Roger, and Nikki remained behind to help out, but the events of the morning had dealt a blow to the celebrations of Christmas.

CHAPTER SIXTEEN

Roger's health

Roger had always considered himself to be one of the healthiest amongst his group of friends. Unlike George who had already had a triple bypass and was regularly consuming numerous medications to combat his high blood pressure, high cholesterol and type two diabetes, Roger was medication free.

He was able, with his medical background, to rationalise that to those many years spent in the Caribbean where diet was restricted and healthy, as most of the food had come from what could be grown locally or harvested from the naturally residing fruit trees and banana plantations. A good dose of sunlight is not to be ignored too, apart from the skin cancer risk, its contribution to vitamin D levels and general stress-free well-being must have had a bearing on his good health.

His annual BUPA full medical checks never saw his blood pressure rise above 129/70 absolutely within normal range and his heart rate at 50 would have served any competitive marathon athlete well.

It was strange therefore that over the past year, he was finding increasing difficulty in climbing stairs and walking down sloping surfaces without a degree of uncertainty. Had he been excessively overweight, at 10 and 1 half stone and five feet eight that was not the case, he would have had an easy explanation for his symptoms. He began to wonder why that was happening and using his knowledge and the considerable expertise of the Google search engine, he set about discovering a medical reason for his symptoms.

Google pointed the way to muscle weakness and the observation that he was experiencing tingling sensations in his toes and fingers to neurological or mycological conditions. Primarily, he came up against Muscular Dystrophy, Multiple Sclerosis and the Polymitotic conditions which gave him an incentive to look further.

Muscular Dystrophy is a genetically inherited condition where the muscles do not develop their full capacity and will usually demonstrate its presence in early childhood. Roger had no familial history to the complaint and only in his late sixties had he begun to suffer from the muscle weakness and atrophy which manifests itself in the young sufferer. He felt confident that he could rule out that condition from his diagnosis for the onset had been too late in life.

He concluded that the manifestation would be a neurological complaint as although there was evidence of muscle wastage, there was also a reduction of motor function; there was lack of muscle power but continued use of those muscles. His preliminary investigations pointed to the need for detailed analysis by appropriate medical specialists.

It is a fact that once you are recognised by fellow medical colleagues as belonging to the profession your access to services becomes rapid and thorough. That is not say that any one of the general public does not

get a thoroughly decent service, but usually the time scale is extended.   Fortunately for Roger, Dr James at the Vale Royal Health centre had become a friend over the years that Roger and Nikki had resided at Wyrevale, and it was to him that Roger turned over his symptoms and suspicions.

Dr James was a likeable individual in his late thirties who had become a regular friend of Roger and Nikki from an initial introduction in the Golf Club. A keen, single figure handicap had placed Dr James amongst the star members of the local club.   Although Roger had never been Golf inclined, the residential status gave him access to the club social facilities and it was through them that his friendship had begun.

Seeking help thus became a matter of a telephone call out of hours and arrangement to meet at the Health centre for further investigations.

The consultation visit went along the same lines that Roger had done in his internet search and the conclusion was that a neurological examination would be the first step in eliminating those conditions thrown up by that process. Roger was duly referred to the local Shire Private Hospital in Warrington.

Dr Davis the Consultant Neurologist was the man to see. He reviewed all the case history and agreed that nerve conductive tests were necessary to seek the possibility of a nerve related condition. These tests involve the passing of electrical impulses along nerve pathways and a study of their speed of transmission. Completed repetitively these can be exceedingly painful and disconcerting when limbs spontaneously move.

At the end of a painful 45 minutes with Simon the quaintly eccentric specialist in such tests, Roger was told that there was in fact a Neurological fault present and that his condition must not be muscle based and would not need any form of muscle biopsy. The wasting and reduction in function could only mean that he had developed Multiple Sclerosis.

There is no quick cure available for that condition and Roger would have to come to terms with his increasing lack of mobility. Decisions were required to accommodate that for future safety and comfort as it was common to experience falls with that condition. Adaptations were needed to the house at Brookdale with its three-storey configuration, not least of which was the installations of hair lifts to allow Roger access to all floors. His office was on the upper floor, and he did not want to lose the view over the 3rd and 5th greens.

Now Nikki was 21 years younger than Roger and up to the date of diagnosis had never considered the age gap to be a problem. The installation of the chair lifts had in some way produced a stigma to the property.

Now with Roger approaching 70 years of age, she was forty-nine, she fore saw a restrictive life ahead or her as his career. That was not how she had imagined her life would be and felt far too young to adopt a lifestyle with so many restrictions. The imposition of these would eat away at her and though she had always loved Roger, a degree of resentment began to creep between them. Why when all the years had treated her so well why was she now placed in that position.

Nikki had been brought up in a devout family on the Island of Dominica where families are traditionally supportive of their elders and the presence of the extended family was commonplace. Although much older, Roger was her husband and not an elder member of an extended family whose respect was guaranteed. She suffered the despair of torn loyalties to a husband and to an elder member of her family, for in England, Roger was her only family.

"But I am still young"

would be the mantra that kept running through her head.

"I am not ready for a restricted life"

"I have much more I want to achieve."

Being torn like that was making a nightmare of her life and she asked Roger before he became too incapacitated to allow her to return to Dominica to try and resolve the anguish she now felt.

Taking the Virgin Atlantic flight from Manchester to Barbados with an overnight stop at the Silver Point Boutique Hotel on the South Coast, she caught the early morning LIAT Dash 8 turboprop to the small Melville Hall airport on Dominica.

It takes one and a half hours to transit the Island back to Roseau, the capital, and the family home.

She had not planned a return flight having purchased an open ticket and would decide when and if she would return once her mind had settled.

Meanwhile Roger was left to fend for himself. At the preliminary stages if his condition he was still able to manage so long as he was careful to avoid the falls which bring not only painful and embarrassing episodes but could place him in a position where he would not recover his upright stance.

Transport was not a problem as the trusty Land Rover was sufficiently equipped with a seat that was at a height to allow easy access and exit without too much effort on his weakening legs. He did worry however as to how long he could manage the manual gear box, so heavy in the Defender, and had decided that an automatic gear change would become a necessity. While Nikki was away, he swapped the ageing Defender for a Discovery automatic, maintaining his lifelong attraction to that manufacturer.

Long distance communication is much easier now in the time of internet-based video calls. His initial daily Skype contact with Nikki soon became once a week as their relationship slowed with the pace of life. Nikki had fallen back into the rhythms of the Caribbean where the sun and sea dictate the slow pace of life.

Her family were initially pleased to see her back but after three weeks were beginning to worry as to the future of her marriage. In such a devout family the prospect of divorce was not considered a reasonable course of action, but they could see her torment and felt deeply for her. Her parents were no longer there, but the aunts and Uncles still played a big part in her life.

Back in Wyrevale, Roger had the support of his friends in the community, but it was mainly George and Amy who stayed connected.

Marriage problems always spread out from the parties involved for it is a human response to veer away from troubles with the difficulty of not quite knowing what the acceptable thing would to say, which one to support and not offend the second individual by that support. For Roger then life became lonelier.

His children from his first marriage had their own lives to live and, in any case, they were not that close both physically and emotionally and the original divorce had placed that gap between them.

George was the mainstay of his support and frequently invited Roger to watch sporting events on TV and Amy would provide supper to feed them both.

Roger however began to wonder what life was all about whether at his age the prospect of living with his condition and alone was worthwhile. The counselling he received contained frequent requests to complete a suicide questionnaire seeking to assure the counsellors that he was not heading down that path.

As a fully qualified medic Roger new extremely well how progressive that condition can be with final loss of the muscles of respiration resulting in death. Would it not better to end it now? He discussed all that with George who implored him not to think that way and seek reconciliation with Nikki.

Nikki had been gone for over three months and had settled in again to the Dominican lifestyle and had begun to meet old school friends who had not been in her calendar for the last fifteen years. Highest amongst them was Godson Robinson a local dental practitioner with whom she had spent most of her teenage years in the Church Bible class.

Godson had qualified at the University of the West Indies in Trinidad and had returned to practice in Dominica where his family had substantial property investments in and around Roseau.

A devout Christian who had never married he was the boy next door that Nikki's parents had always wanted for her, and now that they were no longer present it was her aunts who took control of her life.

They had never approved of her connection Roger and had not been happy when she moved to the UK. They therefore since the new burgeoning relationship had been the former ideal, encouraged the lack of contact with Roger, further fuelling his isolation.

There are 4500 miles separating Dominica from the UK. An eight and one-hour flight to Barbados or Antigua and an Island hoping journey from either on the LIAT Dash 8, these two flights cannot be married, and an overnight stop is necessary, a two-day journey to get there.

Roger had become increasingly concerned that he was losing contact with Nikki, so with special assistance from the airlines set out on that trip without giving fore warning to Nikki, hoping to surprise her on his appearance in Roseau.

Virgin Atlantic only flies to Barbados from Manchester on Sundays. At the beginning of April Roger booked his flight for the 17th to arrive in Barbados at 3.30 that day. He would overnight at the Hilton in Bridgetown and catch the early morning LIAT to Melville Hall airport on Dominica.

During his time at Ross, he had regularly used a taxi driver called Donald to ferry him to and from the airport and he pre-booked Donald to collect him on his arrival.

The flight from Manchester was uneventful and Roger used the business class seat to full advantage, arriving in Bridgetown a little worse for wear. Not normally a drinker, the free champagne had worked its devil magic. The Hilton is set in St James a 20-minute taxi ride from the airport. Jet lag had added to Roger's tired and emotional state as he felt extremely nervous at approaching Nikki in that way.

He would head straight to his room and not wake until 8am the following morning, too late to catch the flight he had booked to Dominica. He was able to acquire a seat on the 3pm flight instead and would schedule to arrive late at Melville Hall on one of the last flights to land before night fall. The airport did not operate after dark.

Morne Diablotins at 4747 feet is the highest mountain on the Island of Dominica and stands in a direct line to the runway at Melville Hall.

Approaching aircraft have to negotiate the eastern slopes in their descent and the winds from the sea, remarkably close to the end of the runway, make that approach necessary.

Occasionally when weather conditions are favourable the aircraft will make a seaward approach but very rarely. On the 18th of April that year the wind direction was such that as the storm clouds gathered over the mountain, the rain become incessant and the pilot had already made two aborted approaches before abandoning his attempt to land and diverted to Antigua, arriving as the light failed, at the much larger V.C.Bird International airport.

It would seem that the Gods were against that reconciliation that Roger was attempting because the only hotel Roger could find a room for the night was at the low-end Jolly Beach Resort. Roger had spent several in Antigua, so the Island was familiar to him, and to have to bed down at Jolly Beach was depressing; further increasing his emotional state.

There were no LIAT seats available to Dominica the following day and Roger had to resort to the much smaller carrier to get him there. Travelling in a small twelve seat Islander is not always pleasant and although these aircraft do good service in and around the Caribbean Islands, they can easily be buffeted by the turbulent air currents that rise above the sea in the large thunderheads which develop many afternoons.

It was one such afternoon when his flight left V.C.Bird and headed for its first stop in Guadeloupe as these small carriers Island hop to maximise their revenues. The normal 40-

minute flight by LIAT was thus prolonged by the smaller aircraft and stops; it was beginning to seem that he would never get there.

The pre-booking with Donald's taxi had been arranged and emerging from the airport buildings Roger was warmly welcomed back.

He had booked a room at the Fort Young Hotel in Roseau and Donald set off on the one and a half hours journey across the Island. It was 5.30 in the evening and the sun had set behind Morne Diabolitin.

Before the major restoration of the road to highway status, the road from Marigot to Roseau was very narrow, potholed and in places only single track wide.

It climbs across the central mountainous range through the Central Forest Reserve and descends very steeply to the west coast. At night, the narrowness of the tarmac and the steep, deep ravines on either side can be daunting.

Donald and Roger had a lot of catching up to do and it was during one of these conversations that Donald's attention to the road was distracted when the large water tanker rounded the bend ahead of them as they entered the village of Pont Casse, producing a jerk reaction from Donald sending his Toyota Minibus over the edge of the road heading for the Layou river at the bottom of the cliff face.

It would be dawn the following day before the bus was recovered half a mile downstream.

CHAPTER SEVENTEEN

Dominica

Dominica records the highest rainfall of any of the Caribbean Islands, with the National Forest Reserve receiving more than three hundred inches a year.

The Layou River has its source high in the reserve which rises more than four thousand feet above sea level; the storms that delayed Roger's arrival on the Island would have contributed considerably to that even during the normally dry months December to April each year.

The Layou River is the longest and deepest river in Dominica, making its way through the Gorge to the Caribbean Sea on the west coast with its mouth close to the village of St Joseph.

After the missing minibus was found in the Gorge, it was easy to identify the missing driver for Donald was registered with the Government of the Island as an official taxi driver.

Donald's fellow drivers and the dispatcher at Melville Hall airport confirmed that he had collected a passenger of European origin on the night the taxi disappeared. The police were thus able to check airline passenger lists and seek out all passengers who arrived that night, checking with local hotels as to whether those passengers had checked in.

They were to discover that one passenger, Roger McNicholl had not arrived at Fort Young Hotel in Roseau; there was no way however of confirming his loss without a body.

As the Layou twists and turns through the Gorge, it leaves deep pools between the areas of shallow rapids, with the storm creating a flash flood it was running much faster and deeper on the night of the incident and so was able to carry the minibus much further downstream than the entry point would have indicated.

The vehicle was discovered in a deep pool where it had become lodged under trees felled by the storm; Donald's body was still inside, but the passenger door was missing and anyone who had been sat on that side would have been lost even though seat belts were fitted to these buses.

Three weeks after the incident no further body had been found, but boys from the village of St Joseph, playing in the shallow waters on the sandy beach of the estuary came across a British Passport floating down stream. It would prove to be Roger's passport.

The police were able to confirm that they now had proof that the passenger lost from the minibus on that night was more than likely Roger McNicholl. No body had been found and would not be as it was assumed that that had been carried out to sea in the fast-flowing flood of the Layou.

Local villagers in the Gorge reported large Anaconda snakes on the banks of the river and were all to ready to put forward the idea that maybe one of these snakes had consumed the body; it was not given any credence by the authorities.

The police had kept a tight rein on information concerning the missing passenger and only after the passport was found did, they release the details to the press. The Dominican, a local news website published details four weeks after the loss of the bus.

ikki who was now enjoying her resurgent life on the Island had been completely oblivious to the incident, but as a regular reader of the

Dominican, she was one of the first to read the press release.

It was met with complete astonishment as Roger had planned his visit as a surprise and she did not know he was coming. To someone who had gone back to her Baptist Faith since arriving from the UK, the news was shocking, and she saw it has an act of God in retribution for firstly abandoning Roger in the UK and secondly for taking up the relationship with her old boyfriend. Her mental health was rocked, and she refused to leave the house in Roseau.

It was her aunt who contacted the local police station and officers were able to come to the house to interview Nikki who was not able to offer any information other than to confirm that the waterlogged photograph in the passport was that of her British Husband.

Back in England, George who had been the prime mover in getting Roger to go and surprise Nikki was seriously concerned that he had had no contact with Roger for over a month. Amy beseeched him to leave Roger alone as probably he and Nikki had reconciled and were too busy enjoying their rejuvenated relationship to bother with anyone else.

The UK press were only to pick up the story once it had been published by The Dominican. Although generally a reader of the Daily Telegraph, Amy would occasionally take the Daily Mail. It was a story contained in that paper with picturesque views of the Layou Gorge, informing that a British Passport in the name of Roger McNicholl had been found, but no body; however, it was certain that Roger had been in the taxi.

George was stunned, as it was his encouragement that had sent Roger there on that fateful trip. It did nothing for his health with an increase in the number of Angina episodes. Amy had had a mobile number for Nikki and although she felt reluctant to use it, George's deteriorating condition stimulated her to make the call.

Nikki, who by now was suffering from a serious case of post-traumatic depression, did not take the call, but her aunt seeing a UK number answered. She was able to explain as much as they knew, and that Nikki was in a bad way mentally and unfit to travel. She realised that there would be affairs that had to be settled in relation to the home in Wyrevale and any will that Roger had left.

Amy agreed to try and contact Roger's children, Dominic, and Samantha, from his first marriage and let them know that in all probability their Father had died in the incident or drowned later in the flash flood of the Layou River.

Roger had re-established his relationship with his children on his return from living in the West Indies and had chosen Wyrevale to be in contact range with them. Although his contact was not on a daily basis, the new beginning was a good one.

Amy and George held a key for Roger's house in case of emergencies and Amy decided to enter in order to find contact information for the children. Roger was meticulous in his office record system, so it wasn't difficult to discover telephone numbers.

Amy invited both children to her house to discuss the way forward as the news of Nikki's mental health, 4500 miles away in the Caribbean, was not moving the resolution of his affairs forward.

CHAPTER EIGHTEEN

Michael and Suzanne Bennett

Michael and Suzanne Bennett had a house on the Lakes. Michael was an ex-professional footballer who had studied law during his playing years in the lower divisions of the Football League and had at one time reached the heady heights of Preston North End. He had begun his career in the Manchester City academy and since his retirement six years previously with recurrent knee problems, he had retained a fanatical allegiance to that club.

Michael was now a solicitor with offices at Gladbrook Park in Northwich, and specialised in sports law, contracts, and sponsorship and management dealings. Suzanne had met Michael during his playing days and was optimistic of becoming a rich WAG, but that never happened, and she was to concentrate her life on their four children, all of whom were under 10 years of age. They both had spent some time living outside Barcelona when Michael had a spell with one of the minor clubs in La Liga.

When Michael and Suzanne moved to Wyrevale, Michael was 40 years old and had hung up his boots six years previously, many of the residents sought his advice on legal matters and although it was not his speciality, he had agreed to draw up wills, Roger's amongst them. On the news of Roger's probable death Michael had instructions to open that will and seek probate. The legal complication was that no body had been found.

The police in Dominica in their attempt to clear up the mystery of the disappearing body had asked for assistance from the Cheshire Constabulary. A specialist diving team was dispatched to supplement the local divers in their search along the entire length of the river from the point of entry of the minibus.

Beginning at the mouth of the river from where the passport had been found, the team grid referenced the search upstream. As that was now the very dry season of early summer the Layou was low in water and many of the deeper areas were now shallower. Numerous deep pools did however remain where the river would bend and carve away at the volcanic rock. Local officers enlisted people who lived along the banks and regularly fished in the waters to identify the larger pools.

On the fourth day of the search in pool more than fifteen feet deep, the divers discovered a suitcase still firmly locked and although full of water it was to reveal clothing and personal effects of Roger McNicholl. That find increased the activity further upstream, but no remains were found.

The information was relayed back to the UK and on to Michael in his attempts to settle Roger's affairs. In the absence of Nikki, he was to ask Dominic and Samantha to his offices to explain the position.

He explained that in all probability Roger was dead, so there would have to be a Coroners enquiry before the will could be read and before probate could be granted. Nikki as next of kin was informed too, but she was still in no fit state to travel.

As a non-working wife, Suzanne had developed a close friendship with Megan since her arrival on Wyrevale, and it was through Megan that she had met Nikki. She was thus overly concerned to hear of Nikki's condition and discussed that with Megan over lunch on the day after Michael had spoken to the children.

They had decided that maybe to help her recovery a visit by both of them to Dominica in support would allow Nikki to come out of her shell. Suzanne however had her four children to contend with, but her mother was extremely willing to lend a hand and cover for a week, but only a week, so the two of them could go to the West Indies.

Amy had supplied Megan with Nikki's contact details and she was able to book tickets for Suzanne and herself on the next Virgin Atlantic flight to Barbados out of Manchester airport. They were to stay overnight at the Hilton in St James and board the next day LIAT flight to Melville Hall on Dominica.

Megan was well travelled and was going nowhere without business class seats; Suzanne, with the drain on income of the four children was reluctant to send the £2500 necessary, but Michael was quick to point out that his fees would cover that, as it was not a simple straight forward will settlement.

There is only one place to stay in Roseau on Dominica if you wish a degree of comfort and not a purely Tourist spot, and that is Fort Young Hotel. Originally a military academy, the building sits on top of a seafront cliff in the capital with open terraces looking west across the Caribbean Sea.

Megan and Suzanne arrived late on Monday afternoon having left Manchester early morning the previous day. The overnight stop in Barbados had been too brief to recover from travel fatigue so an evening collapse was all that could be managed that day.

Waking early the next day the view from their suite was breath taking with the sun rising over the Scots Head peninsula. Suzanne had arranged for Nikki's Aunt Ernestine to meet them at 11am in the relaxed atmosphere of the lounge bar adjacent to the hotel reception. Coffee had been ordered and the three, who initially were stilted in their conversation, would get to know each other once the ice had been broken by Megan with her lilted Welsh accent.

Aunt Ernestine was able to tell then in graphic terms how Nikki had reacted when she read the press release in The Dominican and how she had developed a deep guilt about her actions compounded by the thought of God's intervention and retribution.

Ernestine and her Husband Joshua were the religious couple who were strongly opposed to Nikki's decision to marry Roger all those years ago and more so when she left the Island for the UK. They too believed that some divine intervention had occurred to sever what they believed to be a wrong relationship from day one. It was apparent that they had extraordinarily little sympathy for Nikki in her current state and in a way believed she had received what was due to her for her transgression.

Megan and Suzanne quietly accepted the views expressed by Ernestine and made no attempt to counter them, but once their meeting was over and Ernestine had left, they were free to express how they had felt on its revelations.

Even on the coast in early summer temperatures in Dominica can be as high as 35 degrees and Megan and Suzanne were feeling the effects of the heat and humidity. They decided that to collect their thoughts they need to cool off their anger in the infinity pool on the lower floors of the hotel.

Suitably cooled, with ice-cold Red Stripe in hand, the two of them set to discuss their reaction to Ernestine's position. They decided that they would need to meet with Nikki themselves and make a judgement of the state of mind she was experiencing and come to some decision as to how they could help her regain that spark that they both knew and loved.

They were due to leave from Melville Hall the following Sunday morning in order to be back at Barbados airport for the 9pm return Virgin Atlantic flight to Manchester, leaving then just four days to achieve a resolution. Ernestine had given them permission to visit on Thursday morning; hotel reception had booked a taxi at 10am. The journey to Ernestine's house would take them approximately 30 minutes up the narrow road towards Trafalgar Falls.

The traffic on the road was particularly busy on that day as a cruise ship had berthed early morning. Megan and Suzanne whilst eating breakfast on the terrace, had watched the hordes of American tourists disembark,. The masses then filled a fleet of minibuses for their pre-booked excursions, many to the Falls themselves. Others would depart for the

Emerald Pool or the volcanic mud pools of Soufriere.

Ernestine greeted them politely and showed them to the terrace at the back of the house with its view down the valley over Roseau and out across the Caribbean Sea. Nikki was on a day bed there.

Ernestine:

'Nikki you have visitors'

Nikki:

'I don't want to see the Minister again and certainly not Godson'

At that point Megan and Suzanne entered the terrace. The look on Nikki's face was one of shock and disbelief; whether by guilt or shame she immediately broke down in tears and sobbed and sobbed. That was the first time Ernestine had seen any sign of grief.

Megan and Suzanne were able to calm her down and told her that she should not hold herself responsible for Roger's death, knowing themselves, that to a certain extent the fact that she had left Roger behind and returned to Dominica was the only reason Roger was travelling.

Nikki had to be persuaded to return to the UK to sort out the personal affairs of the marriage and as no body had been found a Coroners hearing to attend. The hearing would attempt to establish a cause of death and issue a death certificate so that probate could proceed. In addition, the life insurance cover which Roger held would not be paid out unless the companies involved had that resolution.

Megan had explained about airline seats for their return flight on which they held one for Nikki. It was hoped that she would be in a frame of mind to travel with them. The flight was on Sunday, that was Thursday, and they had only two further days to get her back from her depression. It was not going to be as simple as that, for Ernestine and Joshua did not want Nikki to leave, for they had seen in her new life back on the Island with Godson and an opportunity now that Roger was dead, that the relationship could become permanent, without the stigma of divorce.

Megan and Suzanne returned again on Friday and Saturday but were still not convinced that Nikki would be joining them on their return to the UK. To get to Barbados for the return flight to Manchester would mean at the latest a departure from Melville Hall at 3pm on the Sunday afternoon; with journey of one and half hours from Fort Young to the airport it would mean leaving the hotel at 12.30pm.

At 11.am they had not heard from Nikki and were packing to vacate their room when a call from reception announced that Nikki was in the hotel foyer.

Megan left Suzanne to finish up and hurried to the foyer. Nikki was there complete with suitcase. She had discussed her future long and hard into the night before with Ernestine and Joshua and at 2am had decided that a return to the UK was the way forward. Should she be able to settle affairs, then there was always the possibility of a return to the Caribbean, her homeland.

In his will, Roger had split his estate in half, giving Nikki the house and income from pensions. The children would receive equally the other half which consisted of numerous investments that he had made during his tenure in Antigua and Dominica. In total these were worth £1.6million. Nikki's share, the house value at £525,000 and pensions at £50,000 per annum was small in comparison but over time would prove to be more.

If you have that level of income and you live in Dominica, then you can live very well indeed for living is cheap and good property cheap too. Should Nikki return with mental faculties intact she would be a wealthy lady.

Nikki left that Sunday with Megan and Suzanne and was never to return.

CHAPTER NINETEEN

Life in Wyrevale

Life never stood still in Wyrevale. While Megan was away, Jez had some very disturbing correspondence from the Inland

Revenue. In its drive to close all loopholes in areas of tax avoidance, and deem it tax evasion, where previously held legal arguments had upheld appeals, the Revenue had sourced some information concerning a company he once owned. Jez had put that company into voluntary liquidation some six years before.

The company supplied nutritional products, protein powders, power bars and anti-dehydration drinks to clients who used his leisure centres. The liquidation had occurred before Jez sold his core business empire. Although that subsidiary fell under the umbrella of the holding company, its separate registration offshore allowed it to be cleanly divorced.

Jez had sourced the products it sold from the USA through Liverpool; what he did not know was these products had originated in China and had been contaminated with lead during manufacture. Several of his health club members who had used the products developed mysterious illnesses which were eventually traced to the protein Powders he had sold as body building stimulants.

Health clubs attract a clientele which will contain a considerable number from the professional classes, lawyers amongst them. When the numbers of individuals who were sub-coming to the condition became noticeably large, one such lawyer realised that there was the potential for mass litigation and money to be made.

Peter Berman was a member of the Health Club in Leeds who began to collect names for a class action against the Nutrition Company and its parent holding company. Fortunately for Jez, the manager of the Leeds branch got wind of Peter's intention and reported that to the management team.

Calling an emergency board meeting, Jez obtained approval to close the company down ahead of the litigation, but in so doing had to dispose of its large cash assets. Dividends were hastily arranged, and the Company liquidated. The litigants were left to pursue the exporter in the USA and through them the Chinese manufacturer

The Nutrition Company had been registered in the Virgin Islands so its ability to dispose of assets to achieve a clear separation from the holding company was the thorn in the side of the Inland Revenue. The company before liquidation had accrued a considerable corporation tax debt and it was that element which had triggered the Inland Revenue interest. They were resolved to dig deep into the background of both Progrow (the Nutrition Company) and Shore Leisure (the holding company).

The Inland Revenue have sweeping powers and once their investigations had begun, they had little respect for social status. Part of their investigation involved a movement of a hefty sum of money prior to the liquidation, and an original deposit when the company was set up and registered offshore. They wanted to know where the money had gone. Why a large corporation tax bill was not going to be paid but more worrying, for Jez, where had the original money come from?

It was clear from their enquiries that Jez had come from that East End criminal background and although not a player, the PR job that Megan's company had done had not managed to completely clear the history.

In the Revenue's view there was no clear source for the start-up capital and questions were asked as to the backers of the Progrow Company. Having his villa on the Costa del Sol with its renowned criminal population did not help for it was assumed that he had that ability to contact and meet with old friends, even new Russian friends who would have money to launder.

Jez had never engaged with any of the underworld in the Costas, but he knew that any investigation would likely throw up that history. He had legitimately financed Progrow from the sale of a BMW franchise which had grown from a small back street garage in the early 1970's, when BMWs were a niche market and not the extremely popular brand of the current middle classes. The franchise had held a branch in Malaga years before too and that had been sold locally in Spain. What he had done however was failed to disclose the profits on that sale to the Spanish Authorities.

He was confident therefore that his background was covered but the transfer of funds before liquidation had to be dealt with.

He engaged a High-Priced Barrister from chambers in Manchester to defend the Company position. That barrister using connections unknown, suspected to be Freemasonry, was able to negotiate a settlement figure with the Revenue for the case to be dropped, it cost Jez £300000, a sum to make most people shudder.

Jez had means to do that and no one would know from where they came. Needless to say, he was not seen on the Costa's for many years to come.

Jez was not the only one having problems whilst the Good Samaritans were away in the Caribbean. Paula and James were locked in a domestic dispute. Paula, having discovered the freedom that her affair with Robert, had given her whilst James was away on his many golf trips, had begun to spend much more time in Alderley Edge. She had changed her outlook on life considerably and that had evoked a visible personality upgrade. Obvious to neighbours, that evolutionary change did not register with James for three months.

On returning from Turkey on his last excursion James expected Paula to be at home to welcome him, but Paula had got the dates wrong and was not expecting James until the following day. When she was not there on his arrival, James called her mobile phone. Receiving no answer, he resorted to an app on both their handsets, which allowed a trace through the GPS. Getting a result for Alderley Edge his mind was alerted to the changes he had begun to notice prior to his departure to Turkey.

Paula received the call and pushing her rustic brown hair from where it was stuck to her face aside, she saw James id, decided to leave the handset alone, not difficult whilst pleasuring Robert with the rising trot she had learnt so many years ago at the Pony Club, much better at it than with your husband at home. It would be necessary however to respond once her breath was back. Hurriedly concocting a story as to her absence, she was unaware that James had tracked her phone to Alderley

Paula's explanation was that she had gone shopping to the Trafford Centre Manchester, with Frankie. She knew she could rely on Frankie to back her up, as Frankie knew of her Robert situation and was so pleased to see the remarkable changes that that had brought to her well-being.

The GPS track would destroy her story and on her return that evening to the house on the Lakes at Wyrevale, a day earlier than she and Robert had planned, James was waiting with the damming evidence. Being the control freak that he was, he could not understand how his power over Paula had been broken and serious and violent questions were to be posed

Paula was no longer prepared to accept his dominance and told him the truth, did not unpack her suitcase, and left the marital home that night. James had his GPS evidence but no knowledge of exactly where or with whom Paula was staying, and as he revealed his means of knowledge, Paula had disconnected her phone.

For several days after Paula's departure, he parked his car on the main road through Alderley in the belief that he would eventually see her, be able to approach her and rectify his problem.

Little did he know that Robert and Paula had left the day after Paula's departure from Wyrevale for Robert's Gite in the Dordogne with no intentions of a quick return. On leaving, Paula had switched her phone back on, placed it inside the chassis of a Waitrose delivery vehicle, and until the battery died James was tracking what he thought were her constant movements around north Cheshire.

Clare and Richard were gradually accumulating more wealth and investing in property, with a particularly attractive holiday home overlooking Lake Vyrnwy in Mid-Wales.

George and Amy were hoping the return of Nikki would solve the increasing worry from the angina attacks he had been suffering since the news of Roger's death. They hoped that the anxiety which had been brought on by the feeling of guilt in sending Roger to Dominica would now dissipate.

Colin and Dina were trying yet another separation but still appearing at social occasions as a couple.

Frankie had yet another failed relationship

Siobhan and Patrick had disappeared with what appeared to be a midnight departure; their home had been sold very quickly, closing off the Governmental attachment. It was rumoured that their cover had been broken and the emergence of new facets of Irish Nationalism could not be ignored.

Life in Wyrevale was thus evolving and the house sales would bring new neighbours for Derek and Michelle. New people whose past was yet unknown but would be revealed as new stories unfolded.

WYREVALE

Book Two

Life Goes On

Chapter One

Life goes on

Roger's death had changed the dynamics of the social group at Wyrevale and with Paula now firmly resident in the Dordogne and Nikki back from Dominica in the Caribbean, the original group had a new look.

Patrick and Siobhan's departure from Devils Rise had brought one of the larger properties to the market, as the first for a long time.

The residents, when making their property purchases in Wyrevale, all assumed that their investment in these properties in the Vale, the common reference, an exclusive residential area, had been a wise decision.

It was a desirable place to live in easy reach of several big cities, Manchester, Liverpool and Chester. It had the added bonus of the

USPGA approved Golf Course, the amenities within the Abbey and the security that a gated community can bring. It was surely a place to attract high worth individuals and their families.

The appearance therefore of a property for sale on Devils Rise, seen as the second-best hamlet behind the Views, because of its height above the valley and distant landscape of the Welsh hills, attracted keen interest. In particular this was applied to the sale value of that property, as this would surely prove them right.

Siobhan and Patrick had been resident as part of the Government witness protection scheme and as such this was concealed from their friends and neighbours. The property had been obtained by an intermediary company on their behalf and this was a front for the secret services.

To keep the confidentiality of this relationship with Patrick and Siobhan, the company was keen to dispose of the property quickly setting the asking price at a level that was not a true reflection of the market price. The witness protection scheme took preference.

They accepted a bid of £520,000 from Greg and Julia, who were to become the new owners. When this was discovered, it would cause alarm from established residents. If this was a true value, then their investment decisions could be challenged.

George, now fully retired, regularly monitored property values within a 10-mile radius from the Vale and was the first to discover the price from Land Registry entries.

He was quick to spread that information amongst his social group, as values were regularly discussed amongst them. The general opinion was that this did not reflect the true valuation, but this was more in hope that they had not made the wrong investment decision.

There must have been an underlying reason for the property to be sold at such a low price.

Was there a structural fault?

Had Siobhan and Patrick trashed the place before they left?

This wasn't clear from the sale particulars that George had obtained and so each member of the Group had a reappraisal of their investment decisions put before them.

Greg and Julia were introduced to the social group by their neighbours Derek and Michelle, as their house although on the opposite side of the peripheral road, was one they regularly visited when previously occupied.

Derek liked to be at the centre of attention and took it upon himself to bring them to the regular Friday night gathering at the Golf Club bar. It was a habit of the group to meet causally on a turn up basis for drinks and bar snacks around 8pm each week.

Those that would normally attend, but not necessarily every Friday, would be Claire and Richard, George and Amy, Michelle and Derek and would have included Roger and Nikki, James and Paula and Siobhan and Patrick.

The group had therefore lost four and as James was now reclusive and at the point of leaving the Vale and Nikki was recently returned from Dominica, two others were in a difficult position.

George was keen to bring Nikki back into the fold, since she had decided not to sell the house on Brookdale following her return and had taken up residence again. Now that she was financially secure, she felt that remaining in the property was a tribute to her dead husband as it harboured many fond memories, even though she had abandoned those a year ago.

She however, needed to source some counselling to adjust her life and deal with the sense of grief and guilt still lingering, in her part in Roger's death. She was aware that had she not returned to Dominica, Roger would not have had to seek her out and therefore would not have been on that road from Melville Hall so late at night.

As Michael and Suzanne had been involved in the management of Roger's affairs it brought them close to Nikki and she became attached to Suzanne, not only for her help in that, but also because of the concern that brought her to the Caribbean, in what she considered to be a rescue mission.

Megan had been part of that missionary attempt but the discovery of Jez's problems with the Inland Revenue on her return had filled her days. Loosing that initial bond that Suzanne had achieved.

Although Nikki was 10 years older than Suzanne the relationship grew and Nikki's lack of children was filled by her interaction with Suzanne's four, adopting them almost as a grandparent. The children came to know her as NaNic.

For Suzanne, this was a God send as she now had a resident babysitter who was dedicated and reliable, living close by on Brookdale. Michael and Suzanne had bought a house on the Lakes just down the stream from Nikki and Roger two years before,

Even though they were close to Jez and Megan who were the pivot of social inter-activity, with their frequent invitations for drinks and nibbles, Nikki became a household friend and neighbour.

The social life of Wyrevale was in the process of change and the newcomers were to inject new energy into the group.

Chapter Two

Michael and Suzanne

Michael and Suzanne were a couple who had moved around many times during their fifteen-year marriage. As a professional footballer, he had to be close to which ever club he was playing for, even though he was not necessarily a regular first team player. Training and coaching sessions dictated his presence at least 3 hours a day every week and more before important matches.

Their move to Wyrevale was their first permanent residence that they could call home base in all that time. Spells with Swindon, Sunderland, Plymouth Argyle and Preston North End, would move the family from one end of the country to another, and the brief spell in the minor leagues of La Liga, with a house in Spain amongst the hills outside of Barcelona.

Not that he played at the Nou Camp on a regular basis, appearing there only once in a cup run, that his minor league team had achieved in his first year with the club.

Michael had a privileged background, for his Father ran a successful Legal Practice in Wilmslow being the Senior Partner in a partnership of six during the developing years of his son's football apprenticeship.

Michael's Father, Gerald, was a keen follower of Manchester City as his parents had moved south from Aberdeen before the second world war, for his Father to play for the club. This connection would allow him to champion them in their rise up the football leagues to become the successful team that they are today. It is a debateable point as to whether that could have been supported without the money from the Middle East.

Michael had attended a minor Public School in Cheadle and had shown a talent for sports, particularly football and lacrosse. Gerald was keen for him to forego his opportunities with Lacrosse, a possible representative position for England, and focus on his football. To reinforce his views, the connections that he had at Maine Road, allowed him to ask a scout to take a look at his son.

The talents that Michael displayed were such that at age 14 he was offered a place in the

Manchester City Academy and Gerald was all too pleased to spend his time driving his son into central Manchester from their home in Bramhall, to take part fully in the regime needed. He saw this as a way to have a much closer relationship with his favourite Club and kudos could be had should his son make the first team.

Michaels true love remained with Lacrosse and his school performances were such, that a considerable number of weekends representing the school and being selected for the county side, became a distraction from his football training. At the age of 16 Manchester City let him go.

The disappointment that Gerald felt at this event would be untold. His determination to get his son into the Football League remained. A fellow student who had studied with Gerald at Universit,y, was the club solicitor for Burnley Football Club and he used this connection to ask the Manager, Jimmy Adamson to look at 16-year-old Michael.

The trial was successful, so at the age of 17 Michael signed semi-professional papers so that he could finish his studies.

His ambition to play Lacrosse for England had to be put aside, squashed by his Father's ambition. Although playing now in division two, following their relegation in 1976, it was thus a good breeding ground for young players.

Gerald knew that any football players' career would be short, never really extending beyond their mid-thirties. There were exceptions of course, goalkeepers such as Peter Shilton with his all-time record number of competitive appearances in world football, would be in his late forties before retirement.

Gerald persuaded Michael to study Law after leaving school, so that he would have a profession to turn to once his playing days were over. As Gerald was a successful advocate, getting his son into Law school was not difficult.

Although dedicated to his studies, Michael's professional football career began at Burnley and it was not long before he was transferred to nearby Blackpool in division two of the football league, as his talents became recognised.

Talents which were not able to stop the relegation to division three in 1978. His Father was still doing the chauffer position to and from Bramhall, until a second attempt secured the driving licence Michael needed and the acquisition of the bright blue Ford Escort gave him independence.

Suzanne was born and bred in Lytham St Anne's, to a family who ran a chain of bed and breakfast hotels along the sea front. Her Mother was the prime mover in this respect and her Father who had once promised to be a successful Police Officer, had taken early retirement and the generous police pension, to help in the family business.

Suzanne had a childhood dominated by her Mother's opinions and did not fully develop her own personality until she was able to escape the closed atmosphere of the family business, with its long hours and frailties of the British weather.

Lytham is known as a retirement town and Jean, Suzanne's Mother, had successfully converted a block of Victorian houses into a retirement home to go with her B & B's. Suzanne at the age of twenty, had been given the job of managing this establishment. Her duties there, and the qualifications she had to obtain to become the manager of such an establishment, gave her little time for a social life and it was rare for her to get an evening out.

One late May Day and completely out of the blue, an old friend from school Charlotte, with whom she had maintained contact, invited her for a night out in Blackpool, those few miles up the coast. She had organised a group of girls from the same class at King Edward VII and Queen Mary School in Lytham. The contrast between the sleepy backwaters of Lytham and the much livelier atmosphere of the Golden Mile was a guaranteed attraction for the group.

Blackpool Town, the football club, had had a successful season in 1976-77 coming to within one point of promotion to Division One. The players including Michael had been given permission for a celebratory night in town after the close of the 1976-77 season. Suzanne and Charlotte and their party were to arrive at the same night club in which the team were celebrating.

Footballers see themselves as local celebrities, a fan base even as small as the crowds at a Blackpool match, would place them there. Many female supporters would act as groupies in this respect, so it was easy for the testosterone fuelled twenty-year-old idols to obtain a one-night stand.

Suzanne and Charlotte and the group of girlfriends were spending a night away from the retirement silence of Lytham and had booked themselves into the Norbreck Castle Hotel on the north shore, not because it had a good review but because the price was low, and they didn't intend to spend much time there. The twenty-minute tram ride would bring them to the centre of town.

The energy of Blackpool at night was a totally different stage to be enjoyed long into the early hours of the morning. Entering a nightclub where the football team's celebrations were in full swing, a group of girls on their own are a certain target for a group of young men, especially if you believe you have something of a celebrity status to support you.

Michael was not the first to approach Suzanne, for as one of the younger members of his party, he was a little over awed by the whole night.

One of his colleagues had already been rejected by Suzanne, but Michael seemed different; more educated, less arrogant with his status. His offer of a cocktail was accepted and more than two hours and several mojitos later they realised there was an attraction between them. So much so that though Suzanne who had no hope of being contacted in her mundane Lytham position, wanted that eagerly to happen.

However, the football season was over, so Michael had until August free before he would have to report back for pre-season training in July. He was therefore free to pursue and spend some of his summertime to entertain Suzanne. She had generally told him that her working week of long hours would make their meeting difficult, but he was determined to see her again.

He had still not moved to live in the Blackpool area, making the daily trip from Bramhall during the season. He began to see Suzanne three times a week, even late at night when she was free, making the journey from Bramhall often arriving at 10pm just to spend in couple of hours in her company.

Suzanne, whose working day began at 8 each morning, was able to catch up on sleep in the brief afternoon lull each day. From the end of May to the end of July they kept the momentum rolling and before Michael started his next season, they had agreed to announce their engagement after the third match, the first at home to Bolton Wanderers, on the 13th of August.

The match was lost 0-1 but their engagement announcement soon pushed this disappointment into the background. Michael would just be approaching his 23rd birthday whilst Suzanne was.

25.

Parents on both sides had been met and been informed. Gerald on Michael's side did not see Suzanne as the girl he had hoped Michael would bring home as a future daughter-in-law, especially as she was older, reluctantly went along with arrangement as Michael's Mother was very enthusiastic and keen for grandchildren.

Michaels playing career did not hit the First Division of the Football League, no Premiership in those days, as Gerald had hoped and the season 1977-78 was a disaster for Blackpool.

After their relative success the previous year, they were relegated to the third division for the first time in their history. This demotion spurred Michael to move clubs and his transfers over the next 8 years, around the country and into Europe meant that his Mother or a Grandmother as she would become, did not see the grandchildren as often as she would wish.

The first grandchild, Sylvia, had been born when Michael and Suzanne were in Spain when perhaps. Michael at 26, was at the pinnacle year of his career, if however small. The time spent there would only be too short for he was released at the end of a two-year contract which had been plagued with injuries.

He returned to England to be approached by teams in the lower divisions, but recurrent knee injuries would call an end to football at age 33. He was glad therefore he had taken his Father's advice and obtained his Law Degree.

Gerald saw the connections that his son had developed through his sporting career as an opportunity to develop his Law Firm in the area of sports contracts and offered Michael a position in the practice.

It did not take long for Michael to realise he could not collaborate with his Father and once established in his speciality, Sports contracts and agencies, he set up his own practice in Northwich on a newly developed business park.

Centrally positioned in the triangle between

Liverpool, Manchester and Birmingham, his client list would develop much wider than football alone. Lower division football teams were nearby, Chester City, Tranmere Rovers, Crewe Alexandra, Wrexham with Shrewsbury

Town not too distant. He was however keen to diversify and called on his past achievements to promote the new company.

Established in Northwich with his law firm, the development of Wyrevale centrally placed in Cheshire, seemed a place to set down roots with Suzanne and the children, for now there were four in tow, Sylvia, Johnathan, Amy and Gordon. Why they chose the last name when his surname was Bennett, only they knew, but they were to set him up for much ridicule in the future.

The house on The Lakes was set on the side where the stream joined the lake that backed onto the 16th green, and its construction made use of this aspect to the full. Balconies on the first floor off the master bedroom, gave an excellent view of the hole from its tee to the 456-yard green. Doglegging toward the houses and stream, the temptation to high handicap golfers was to cut the distance by playing over the hill rough on the right, a blind shot, much like the Road Hole at St Andrews where the best line is taken over the hotel,

Low handicappers would struggle to make four, the par and although beautifully positioned for the view, many of the houses received golf balls into their gardens, when the first shot was hit too long. This was a price to pay for their position.

Michael and Suzanne had purchased number three, two down from the bridge which crossed the stream so well out of range of this distraction and Nikki was across the stream which divided Brookdale in two halves, at number 17. Her back-garden view was of the short par three third hole green, beyond the small stand of beech trees planted as part of the overall landscaping of the Vale.

The stream that separated the two parts of

Brookdale had small pedestrian bridges at the Abbey end to allow foot traffic between the club house and the first hole, and another at the approaches to the 17th green. Although non-golfers were not allowed on the course, there were public footpaths that provided attractive pathways around the landscaping, much used by the keep fit fanatics on their jogging/running laps.

Michael because of his knee injuries had given this up but Suzanne who was keen to keep her figure trim following her four pregnancies, could be seen on her daily run each morning once the children had left for school.

She was regularly joined by Nikki who had always maintained a good figure and now that she was approaching fifty, she was forty-seven, was determined not to gain that midlife spread. Her natural rhythmic stride was more than a match for the efforts of Suzanne, whose style was not so fluid, for their daily meetings encouraged the friendship between them and the connection with the children.

Michael's business was going from strength to strength even though he dealt with the minor leagues of the professional game, the fact that he became an agent for many up-and-coming players allowed him to benefit from their transfer fees as they moved upwards.

The houses on Brookdale were generally smaller than the other properties on Wyrevale, but the position of the Bennetts house on the Lakes was such that overlooking the 16th green gave them the largest plot and biggest property in that hamlet.

The golf course had been adopted by the lesser-known professional tours and would hold competitions on that tour which Suzanne and Michael exploited by inviting their friends to watch from the large balcony, which extended over the garage complex, from their master bedroom. This was large enough to set up a barbecue and drinks table to supply needs whilst whiling away an afternoon in hopefully, the sunshine.

Michael was particularly adept at the barbecue and would display his talents in many ways. The envy in this respect of many present, particularly George, he would rustle up burgers, sausages and steak without a sign of confusion, perfect timing so that everything arrived together along with the grill roasted vegetables.

His particular speciality was whole chicken cooked over a can of beer, bubbling internally, which delivered moist and tasty meat cooked from the inside and from the grill on the outside.

The ladies of course would consume numerous bottles of wine, discussing their latest brand and where to obtain the best deal. Even though Sainsburys were offering six bottles for 25 pounds, the discount store supreme was a better buy.

Amongst the men, talk ranged from the golf taking place before them, and of course with Michael's connections, football dominated the banter. Although Michael had been part of the Manchester City Academy and rejected, his loyalties remained with that club.

Jez, although his London Connections were in the East End, was a Tottenham supporter and George had developed a business connection with Manchester United in his working days, despite being based in the Southwest of England. The one fanatical supporter of Liverpool, Patrick with his Irish roots, had now left so a vacancy was there to be had.

When Greg and Julia arrived on the Vale, and Derek introduced them, that gap was filled. Greg's Father had been born in Liverpool, only moving to Worfield in Shropshire in his late teenage years there to marry Greg's Mother and assume permanent residence. Even then, distant from the city, his support for Liverpool remained strong. Greg's allegiance was thus inherited.

Julia had forgotten the connection that her deceased husband had with Stoke City, but amongst the banter being loudly pursued on the balcony, his tragic death surfaced and, in a way, provoked a feeling of guilt, for now she was enjoying her new life so much without him. This was a secret that the Vale Group had yet to discover.

As the sun set behind the hills in the distant Welsh borders, the party was in full swing and as the temperatures faded with the dying ambers of the light on the horizon, the party retired indoors. Everyone knew that drink and driving was a not an ideal but the private roads on the Vale were often used to transport several inebriated drivers and their passengers around the peripheral road back to their respective hamlets. Nikki of course had just to walk across the bridge over the stream. Many a sore head would be raised from the pillows the following morning.

All the residents of the Vale had social membership of the golf club and on Sunday mornings, to encourage the golf members, the Club had breakfast available from 8am to 11am.

With a sore head and the prospect of cooking not desired, several party members would use this facility to try and calm their stomachs with a full English. Bacon from the local Deli, black pudding, mushrooms, hash browns, eggs and tomato accompanied as much toast as you could eat; sufficient, if taken close to the 11am deadline, to be regarded as brunch and set up for the day.

Nikki had joined Michael and Suzanne with their children at 10.45 and declined the Full English for a continental basket of pastries and strong black coffee. She had taken far too much wine the previous night and her Caribbean, Baptist upbringing had never introduced so much alcohol to her before. The children although normally well behaved were particularly noisy that day, and despite Suzanne's attempts to rein them in did not help to dispel the numbness in Nikki's head.

Jez and Megan appeared at five to eleven just catching the chefs before they closed the breakfast menu to begin lunch time preparations. Neither seemed worse for wear, as the party lifestyle they had enjoyed whilst London based, had conditioned them in many ways with alcohol and the no longer mentioned drug habits. Jez from his athletic background had resisted this, but Megan had been a frequent user of recreational cocaine, regarded as not essential in the social circle of Cheshire and her habit had declined with their move north.

Derek and Michelle did not appear and so the gossip round the table revolved around Derek's behaviour the previous evening.

Derek had a sensible limit of two pints, but as the beer was free flowing had greatly exceeded that. A man who liked to hear the sound of his voice and very opiniated he would argue black was white if needed. During the evening the male banter had developed into a discussion of the relative value of professional footballers and the wages they received. Michael of course with his professional life so closely related to this subject was keen to get his point across but had been shouted down by Derek on many points.

So loud did the discussion become, that Suzanne with Michelle's help, tried to intervene where upon Derek turned his attentions to her. Without thinking it through he began to ask what she knew about the subject, as she was only a stay-at-home pampered wife. This was too much for Michael who asked Derek to leave. He was not eager to do that, and it was only with Michelle's forceful voice that she managed to get him out of the house.

Derek and Michelle's invitations were to suffer inconsequence and they became a peripheral couple in the group. Derek was still a golf club member, and it was seen that they began to socialise with different members of that club and not necessarily residents of the Vale.

Chapter Three

Greg and Julia

The sale of Siobhan's and Patrick's former house on Devils Rise had gone through so quickly that the new occupants Greg and Julia were resident some four months after its placement on the market. Everyone in the remaining social group, agreed that they had been able to obtain a six-bedroom, three story property at a knock down price. This was more in expectation that their own properties were of greater value than perceived from the price paid by Greg.

Within the resident group, Jez and Megan, Derek and Michelle lived on Devils Rise where twenty houses had been built on the sloping ground amongst the pines and took advantage of the natural surroundings on the hill side. The ring road ran between the two sections of this hamlet, with those houses situated above the road considered to be the ones to have.

Jez and Megan occupied one of the better, larger plots whilst Derek and Michelle who featured on the lower side of the road had paid less for their house. Michael and Suzanne on the same side as Jez and Megan had paid the same amount, which more than reinforced the bargain they had obtained in Pinewood Close.

Derek was not a man to hold back in the quest for inside information on any new arrivals and particularly in this case where he felt he had been cheated on price. He became anxious to establish the background to the new residents. Before his ejection from Michael and Suzanne's house he had long conversations with both Greg and Julia and had become very conversant with their background.

Julia, who had two late teenage daughters, Polly 17 and Carly 19, had been widowed since the youngest was nine, when their Father was involved in a multi-car accident on the M6 just past the Sandbach Services. His bright red Jaguar XJS had submarined under a

Polish sixteen wheeled articulated lorry which had blown tyres and jack-knifed in front of him. The following six vehicles compounded his position and only after the emergency services had removed them were they able to remove his much-damaged body from under the lorry.

A keen football fan of Stoke City, he had been to see them play Manchester United one weekday night. On his return home, the fog was very thick between junction 17 and 16, a contributing factor to his accident. In view of the weather conditions, the air ambulance had not been available and the slow journey to hospital did not help his chances to survive. He later died in Stoke Royal Infirmary of multiple injuries.

Julia, the two young girls and Andrew (Andy) lived in Trentham, a smart suburb of Stoke on Trent, from where Andy ran a business selling caravans and motor homes in the nearby town of Stone. A very successful business man, he was a keen golfer and a member at Trentham Golf Club. Following Andy's tragic accident, Julia had to take on the reins of the business and continued to be successful at that.

The girls were able to attend Ellesmere College for their secondary education, set in that small Shropshire town across the county border. Although it was possible for them to attend as day pupils, Julia's busy life in the business made the opportunity for them to board, a release from trying to juggle family and business life.

Her business was going strong, and the school fees could easily be met and in true sense the school experience was much better as a boarder, for they were able to take part in after school activities.

Ellesmere, as a school. is extremely well equipped to provide a wholesome education and it was obvious to anyone who met the girls in their teenage years that they had benefitted greatly from their time there.

Julia had trained as nurse in her late teens and early twenties but with the help of her parents and with the pay-out of the large life insurance following Andy's death was well set in life financially.

Although her business was successful, she yearned to return to her earlier career, which she felt was her vocation.

She was able to dispose of the business within two years of the accident and with-it memories which she felt could be better left behind for she needed to move forward in life.

She returned to nursing and became a specialist MacMillan nurse at what was once Stoke City General Hospital.

Greg who suffered from testicular cancer had been admitted to the chemotherapy unit in the City General and had been counselled during his stay by Julia. Greg had to suffer the indignity of not only losing his hair but also the discovery that whilst in the throw of treatment, his wife had been having an affair with his best friend John.

Barbara, his wife, said that she could not come to terms with the fact that her husband was about to lose his male gonads but could not grasp that this, not necessarily meant a future with no sexual activity, at which she had been regularly active and wished to continue.

Greg could not forgive her and had sought a quick divorce to get rid of the woman who had let him down in a very big way, in his time of need. Fortunately, they had no children to drag into this mess.

Following his discharge from hospital, Greg had approached Julia, socially, in the hope that he could arrange an evening out to thank her for all her care during his stay in hospital.

The medical profession is very strict on the interaction of practitioners and patients, and it is considered unethical to have relations with a patient. It is easier to survive a death of a patient at your hands than to have a sexual relationship with your patient.

Greg however was now discharged, and Julia no longer had a professional context with him, so when he called, for he had obtained her number during counselling in case of an emergency, she was able to take the call.

It was years since she had been on a 'date' and during that time she had dedicated herself to getting back into nursing, and for several years had still grieved the death of her former husband, spending as much time with the girls as possible before sending them off to boarding school. This she felt filled a hole in the family life left after her husband's death.

Julia's Mother was pleased to hear that someone had asked her out, for she felt that it was time Julia began to have a life beyond work and the family, although surprised to hear Greg was younger than Julia, encouraged her to go.

At the second time of asking, Julia plucked up enough courage to go, for at 43 years old the concept of dating seemed so much an event of bygone years. Even with her deceased husband, Andy, there was never an occasion that appeared as a pre-arranged date as they had been at school together and teenage sweat-hearts.

The day dawned when she had to get ready to meet Greg for the first time since their professional contacts several months before, in a nurse/patient relationship. Proving a nerve racking sensation, her mother had come to take care of the dogs, to give Julia encouragement and a confidence boost before Greg arrived. There were two dachshunds in the household, who as young puppies had to be chaperoned to stop destruction of the stair case,

Greg called at the house in Trentham around 7.30 and had booked a table for dinner in Eccleshall at Julian's restaurant, to which he had received excellent reviews. Conversation in the car, a Mercedes E-class, for the 10-mile drive was a little awkward and stilted, but once settled at their table they began to exchange life stories.

Once settled with a Gin and Tonic for Julia and a Ginger Beer for Greg, he was driving, the menu selected, and excellent food served the evening became more relaxed. The time sped by, and Greg dropped Julia back at the house at around 11.30. There was a mutual agreement that they would like to do this again.

–

Greg prior to his cancer had lived in Stockton Brook, just off the Leek road from Stoke-on-Trent and ran a small garden nursery with several acres. Whilst undergoing his hospital treatment, he had managed to obtain planning permission for the development of a fifty-house estate on the land behind the nursery and closed a sale of the complete site to Taylor Woodrow for £15 million pounds.

As a consequence, he no longer needed the nursery which was sold separately making him comfortably off now during his recovery. He no longer needed to work even if he could, obtaining an apartment in Newcastle-under-Lyme, he joined the Trentham Golf club, enjoying a return to his childhood prowess on the greens.

The affair that his wife had had whilst he was in hospital had triggered the divorce at which a settlement was achieved before his windfall sale of the business. His settlement had been based on the earlier performance of his company in years past, which had not always been that good, but it meant Barbara keeping the house in Stockton Brook.

He was able to fend off further demands following the sale of the land as this had been obtained with a loan from his parents and in effect belonged to them. The disposal of the nursery for a relatively small sum did form part of the settlement as she had in some way contributed to the growth of that in its early years.

Following the completion of the divorce settlements, his parents who had not been in good health, both in their late seventies, had recently died within a few weeks of each other. The land at the back of the nursery, which they owned came as an inheritance. The divorce settlement had been agreed and the absolute obtained prior to this event and was thus considered exempt from that.

Greg was not a local lad. He originated from a small village outside Bridgenorth in Shropshire called Worfield. Not a large place but a hotel and two pubs with the Golf club across the main road provided a tight knit community. As a small boy, he had shown a developing talent at sports and had been encouraged by his parents to join the junior section in the Golf Club. By age 14 he had a handicap of ten and regularly played in the regional junior championships during which he was able to examine many qualities of the courses and admired the work that the green keepers displayed, for the family business was in gardening.

As his schooling progressed his interest in the up keep and maintenance of each course turned his interest to horticulture. He was able to get a place at the then Harpers Adams College, now University in nearby Newport, to study grass technology.

On graduation, he was however to discover that opportunities were few and far between for a young green keeper and as his parents already owned a small garden nursery, he chose to use his knowledge in that direction.

Whilst at Harpers, Greg had met his future wife Barbara and at the tender age of 23 and on graduation they had become engaged. Barbara came from Stoke-on-Trent where her parents were schoolteachers. Barbara who was a keen horse woman, who had thoughts of becoming a Farmer, had attended briefly at Harpers on a one-year foundation programme in Agriculture. Her school qualifications were not good enough to qualify for the degree courses. To her dismay there was far too much Mathematics to address and at the end of the first year she had not obtained the

40% pass mark to continue further with her studies.

She did however meet Greg and their relationship grew during that single year and continued through the completion of his degree course.

When they decided to announce their engagement, decisions were required as to where they should live.

Barbara had returned to live with her parents in Stoke-on-Trent and the many visits that Greg made to their house in his battered Land Rover, during the formative years of the relationship, had made that the direction in which his future would go ahead.

He was able to take a position with Stoke-on-Trent City Council in their Parks department and took on the management of those recreational areas just before his 28th birthday. They were able to set up home in Kidsgrove not far from where Barbara's parents taught school, his daily commute into the city was relatively easy.

Three years working for the council was enough for Greg who felt restricted by budget cuts, so when the opportunity arose to buy the small nursery, a return to his childhood upbringing, he persuaded his Parents to help financially in the acquisition.

Greg now thirty-one was the new owner of the Elem Nursery and Garden centre lying between Norton and Leek. He was ambitious in their management and with his University degree behind him, was soon changing things and enlarging the premises at which he became successful. It did however require a considerable amount of his time and it was not unusual for him to work long hours approaching 16 hours a day at weekends, his busiest time.

Although Barbara enjoyed the increased wealth during their close relationship in their early years of marriage, this began to wane and with the long hours of Greg's absence. In her life she was lonely.

Initially the growth of the business was good but when the national economy took a downturn, Greg's financial commitments that had fuelled that early growth began to have a stranglehold on profits.

In his years from 35 to 38 the profitability fell by 50% increasing the gap between his wife and himself, for she no longer had access to the lifestyle previously enjoyed. Not even the fine house bought in Stockton Brook when they were both thirty-five helped in this way, for the mortgage was now a family burden.

Barbara was an individual whose glass was always half empty reflecting a negative few on life.

Nothing was good enough, the house wasn't big enough and needed her constant attention, their social life was not active enough and everything she wanted had to happen now, it could not wait.

Greg was suffering from the total negativity although he did not realise his depression, the stresses and strains, took its toll on Greg, culminating in his diagnosis with cancer very early in life.

The evening at Julians for Julia, was the start of many evenings spent together and their relationship grew sufficiently for Greg to suggest a weekend away in Venice. In all her travels with Andy in her previous marriage, Julia had never been to Venice, and it had been on her wish list. Her daughters encouraged her to go as she had not had a holiday in the last eighteen months.

Taking the Monarch Airlines flight from

Manchester Airport to Marco Polo airport in Venice, Greg and Julia took a water taxi across the lagoon to enter the city down the Grand Canal.

It was all it promised to be from the pictures in holiday brochures. The architecture, the gondolas, and frequent journeys of the water buses, the Vaporetti, the place was alive. As they disembarked alongside the Rialto Bridge, Julia was in heaven.

A short walk through the narrow streets saw them arrive at their hotel only a few hundred yards from St Mark's square. It would be the first time they had shared a bedroom.

Not in the last 10 years had Julia undressed before a man, so after dinner that evening, taken in one of the small restaurants on the canal side, the return to the bedroom and the prospect of sleeping together played on her mind.

Could she remember how to do it?

Would it be a disaster?

What to wear between the sheets?

Greg, ever the gentleman was aware of Julia's nervousness and allowed her to use the bathroom first so that when she was finished, she could already be in bed if she so desired and as discreet as she wanted to be.

Greg turned out to be the gentlest of lovers, and Julia, 10 years since her last encounter, was to experience a sensation she had almost forgotten, that heady rush of pleasure which could almost blow the top of the head off.

That pleasure was repeated more than once during that first night and would continue over the three days of the break in that most romantic of cities.

Venice is too nice a city to spend all your time in bed, so between their passionate episodes they strolled the streets, dined in canal side restaurants, took a Gondola ride, and even splashed out on coffee on St Mark's square at 17 euros a time.

All too soon the weekend was over and, on the flight, back to Manchester, Greg asked Julia if she would consider their relationship a permanent one.

Julia, full of emotions from the weekend was tempted to say yes straight away but her head caught her heart before she responded. She would have to talk it over with the girls, respect their views and speak to her mother, but if all agreed then yes, on one condition that they moved away from memories past and started with a clean slate.

Julia's Mother was a little surprised that this had happened so quickly but could see the new sparkle in Julia's eyes and the overall improvement in her view on life, that this relationship was good news.

The Girls were summoned home for the weekend to receive the news. They too could see the changes in their Mother's joy and although they had had little contact with Greg as boarders at school, had an immediate sense that this was the right thing for their Mother to do.

To celebrate the overall agreement, Greg booked a holiday in Tenerife, and again Julia's girls encouraged her to go and get some fun back into her life after 10 years of bringing them up.

Greg booked a room for 14 days at Iberostar Grand Hotel Salomé - Adults Only in Costa Adeje for the two of them. Julia was conscious that this would be the second time they shared a bedroom and now that the 10 years that she had not slept with a man were over, she knew that worries on her lack of recent training would no longer be there.

The Monarch flight, this one from Birmingham airport arrived on time and their pre-booked private transport whisked them away in Mercedes comfort to the hotel.

Checking in was simple but Julia's nerves were on edge. They followed the porter to their room where she discovered that Greg had booked a suite for the glorious sea views of the Atlantic rollers after their 3500-mile journey from the Caribbean.

Greg ever the gentleman suggested they unpack and retire to the bar for a sunset gin and tonic, as this was Julia's desired way to spend that time of day.

Sitting on the terrace with the sun slowly sinking into the Atlantic they both began to relax, helped enormously by the Bombay Sapphire and Schweppes Indian Tonic.

At 6.30 they agreed to retire to the suite and change for dinner. Julia had brought a red dress especially for this event and proceeded to prepare herself for the evening. Greg chose the casual attire of pink linen trousers and a white cotton shirt over his Cole Haan loafers, without socks of course.

Dinner was served on the terrace with evening temperatures in the high 20's Celsius the cool breeze was a blessing. The five-star hotel was ranked highly for its food and Chief Chef Almondo was on good form. Three hours flew by, and the wine was pleasant.

The nerves between them melted away with the good food and the cabernet sauvignon.

Taking the evening slowly they retired to the bar for after dinner drinks in some way delaying the return to the bedroom. Julia's girls had persuaded her to buy a complete set of new underwear and night clothes so as she returned from the bathroom, she had put on a black silk night dress to impress.

Greg however was used to sleeping naked and was standing admiring the night view from the balcony windows. Although he had not worked for several months, he had kept the toned body of the former garden nursery worker used to strenuous manual labour.

Although fading after his time in hospital, the tanned legs and arms of the shorts wearing outdoor life contrasted with his pale torso. As he turned away from the window to greet Julia, it was obvious that he was pleased with what he saw.

His once calloused hands from years of manual labour, were now soft again after his months of treatment and convalescence, and their gentle circling of the soft down around her navel was all that was needed to smooth away any remaining nerves that Julia had still built up.

Before Julia's acceptance of his proposal, Greg had been searching for properties that would suit them all, and when Julia's condition of relocation was put forward, he was readily armed with suggestions, as he was prepared to take the girls on board and the property at Wyrevale with its bargain price filled the bill.

The former house of Siobhan and Patrick on Devils Rise, beautifully decorated and well-maintained garden, the view down the valley to the Welsh Hills and its high standard of upkeep, made the purchase a relatively easy one. Little did they know that all that high standard had been put in place by the secret service once Patrick and Siobhan had left. The price was well within the means he had available.

Julia, Greg and the girls moved in three months after the holiday in Tenerife.

Chapter Four

James

Following the removal of James from the Golf Club Captaincy as a consequence of his accident in the car park, and his break-up with Paula, James had become reclusive. Even though Paula was now established in her new life in France, in the village of Sarlat, many of their Wyrevale friends had sided with her during the split and they still held the view that it was James who was the main culprit for her move away.

Living alone in the large five-bedroom house by the Lakes, he would only be seen on the Golf course where he had had to find new playing companions amongst the newer members who were not party to past events. How he kept them secret no one knew.

The house was far too big for a single individual, and he was keen to downsize, for the up-keep of the garden was becoming a chore.

Placing the property in the hands of an Estate Agency in Manchester, he hoped to attract a buyer who was prepared to commute or could happily manage their business from Wyrevale. In so doing he expected a higher valuation.

Properties of this type available, particularly with the views of the Lakes and combined with the Golf Course attached, were very rare in the nicer suburbs of Manchester. Those that were on the market were much more expensive, so James thought the £850,000 asking price was good value.

His view was supported by the rapid finding of a buyer who was prepared to pay the asking price, and James moved off the development. In a way, this was a reversal of the pathway which had got him in a position to buy number 10 The Lakes in the first place.

James had begun life after graduating from Nottingham University with poor grade business degree and began life working for the council in Leicester. Living with his first girlfriend, Sonia who he had met at

University, he managed the trade waste collection service and maintenance of public conveniences. In that job he gained IT knowledge during these early years. Which allowed him to change direction.

He obtained a job for a large American software company. His position was one of a trouble-shooter, being called in to manage projects that were stalled or looking bad. After sorting out the IT for a small company in Devon and Cornwall who supplied cleaning products. His investigation of their business had made him realise the potential in this field and his understanding of the world environmental protection programme and cleaning services, obtained during his position with the council, would eventually encourage him to seek his own business in that trade. Sonia didn't view his position as particularly glamorous and contrasted with her own career pathway with Boots.

James felt if he was to use his gained knowledge further, he needed to move to that arena. When a commission only job was advertised for a cleaning product salesman, and much to Sonia's dismay he applied and was given the job. The position offered a doubling of his salary from the Council, less than his IT position but a company car and on target bonuses. What he failed to realise was that to achieve this would mean many hours on the road and away from home.

Sonia became disenchanted with this life, and when James discovered her affair with the husband of an ex-school friend. James had sought the break to clear the air and allow him to take a second look at his business career.

Apart from his Council experience and the brief IT job, he had spent the last three years lugging a grey Audi A4 estate full of cleaning products, up and down the motorway system of England and Wales with the occasional ferry to Northern Ireland.

During that time, however he had increased his knowledge in that field. Now free from Sonia he was able to choose his own future and on reading an advert in the trade magazine for a small cleaning company in Sandbach, Cheshire on the redeveloped former Foden Lorry factory, he obtained funds to complete the purchase. This of course meant a move away from Leicester. He bought a small house in Elworth on the out skirts of that historic Cheshire town.

The move was a complete success for within two years he had doubled the turnover of the company, paid off the bank loan and profited from the long-dedicated hours he had put into the company growth.

His single existence and long hours on the job had removed the extra waist line weight once collected in his travelling salesman days and he returned to his youthful toned figure developed with the exercise on the Golf course. He had not taken a holiday in all that time. He was now 35 years old.

James had been born in Leicestershire in a small village, Ratcliffe on the Wreake; his parents were butchers in nearby Melton Mowbray famous for its Pork Pies. Close to where they lived, the Beedles Lake Golf Course was the club to which his Father had belonged. James, who during his teenage years could regularly be seen on the fairways, was moderate player at this time. He continued to play throughout his University years and maybe devoting more time to this than his studies, was responsible for his poor results.

It could also be a consequence of the party lifestyle he lived whilst in Nottingham and his experimentation with recreational drugs. His use of Marijuana was a regular habit which he carried forward into his first relationship, much to Sonia's disgust, and this combined with the long hours on the road during the week, and golf at the weekend were the contributing factors in their split.

When James moved away to his new life in

Cheshire his habits went with him. Living alone for the two years establishing his new business, stresses and strains were relieved by a joint or two, and with his increasing wealth, the introduction of cocaine.

His Golf continued too, for now there was no one too complain about the long weekend hours spent on the greens and the 19th hole.

James had achieved a handicap of seven during his playing at Beedles and he found the local courses in Cheshire not challenging enough so became a member at Carden Park on the road to Wrexham. Here he had the chance to play two courses, the old Cheshire Course and the Jack Nicholas designed, Nicholas Course. He had gained membership after it had been opened by Jack himself and Ian Woosnam.

It was twenty-five miles from home, but now that he had acquired the BMW X5 he found that driving was a pleasure.

Two years without a holiday had begun to wear him down so in the summer of 2000 he booked himself in to the 5-star Marriott's Marbella Beach Resort for there were two golf clubs within 1.9 miles of this highly recommended hotel. It was during this holiday that his future was to take a turn in a different direction when he met Paula, she was 24 years old.

The quick romance and early marriage had brought Paula to Cheshire from the family home in Worthing and although many miles distant, and much derided nationally, the luxury reputation that Cheshire had, suited her background. The daughter of a former stockbroker who had received a private education, finishing her schooling years at a Roedean, had taken a place at Reading University to study business and IT management where she obtained a 2.1 degree.

On leaving Reading her early work was with

American express in Brighton which gave her the CV on which she was able to obtain the position with Barclays at Radbrooke Hall on her move North. To sweeten the move from her home James had purchased the house on the Lakes which served the dual purpose of a new pasture and maintained his close interest with Golf.

Paula knew James played Golf, as their initial meetings in Spain had occurred when James was on a Golfing Holiday, but she never imagined that he would spend many hours following his hobby. Nor was she fully conversant with his drug usage for when in Spain this had not been visible and in the early months of their engagement was kept well hidden.

Although long separated from his first girlfriend, James had stayed connected with her during his last two single years and occasionally met with John and Sonia on social events back in Leicestershire. This connection remained following his marriage to Paula and may have been part of the early discord between them. Neighbours on Wyrevale could not see reason to this continuation of an obviously broken relationship.

Paula's first marriage was to a family friend, Alan who had been singled out by her parents as the suitable candidate for their daughter. It was not an arranged marriage but for all accounts and purposes it could have been. Alan's parents played golf with Paula's at Hill barn Golf Club outside Worthing, and it was set up there.

Being a keen student at Reading University, Paula chose to stay close to home during her University years and travelled back each weekend the 70 miles from her flat near the Royal Berkshire Hospital. The flat was an investment her Father had made once she had obtained a place in Reading.

Living alone there and going home each weekend left her out of much of the University social life and being a basically shy individual, the familiar surroundings back in Worthing were easier to manage. She would therefore miss out on the complete education a University has to offer with these extra-curricular activities so much part of that whole package.

Living at home was much easier and had the journey to Reading been much smaller it would have been doubtful if she would have taken up the flat in the first place.

Social contacts were always made through her parents, so the introduction to Alan and the expected development of that relationship was determined by her choice to return home each weekend.

Both sets of parents had expectations, and despite her Father's reservations, following her graduation, she would marry Alan. He had forsaken a University place to accept a position in his Father's family business supplying paper to the printing industry. A position that kept him in close contact to Worthing.

Initially, the marriage seemed to be successful, but as Paula's career with American Express took off, she began to outstrip Alan both intellectually and emotionally. Alan wanted children early in their marriage, but she was not in favour as she developed her new found personality through work, seeing the presence of children as a distraction from her personal growth. Within 3 years the heated arguments bore their toll and Paula wanted out. She was twenty-four.

No one else took part in the split and much to her Mother's despair, no children involved. Paula walked away from the marriage. Her Father, who all along had not seen Alan as the best match was quietly pleased.

Paula remained living with her parents, part of the return generation, and worked her way up the ladder at American Express and with that connection, a social life with the girls she worked with.

The group had planned a holiday in Spain, Paula included, where upon she was to meet

James. Fifteen years later she was in the middle of another marital split, but she was so much in love with Robert that this was all consuming.

–

James sold the house on the Lakes to a lady who was based in Hale, a rich suburb of Manchester, who he believed wanted to move away from the city and take a more gentle, rural existence.

Shortly after the sale completion, decorators were seen to move in, and the gardens again became manicured. For the neighbours, Alex, and Joan, were to inherit different neighbours and new occupants.

It was clear that the two women who lived there, it was assumed they were sisters, had visitors who were many and varied. Vehicles parked in the drive would change for Audi to Mercedes, Bentley to Jaguar and never for prolonged periods.

The Lakes had been designed so that each property had its own plot backing on to the water with planted trees defining the individual boundaries, so that privacy for each plot was achieved. To view from one house to the next would require a determined effort to see through the trees.

Rumours began to spread at the Friday night Golf Club meet, that all was not as it seemed at number 10. The visitors were too frequent and varied and the two female occupants rarely ventured out of the house, apart from the regular deliveries of food by Ocado, it was wondered how they survived.

The Lakes house designs had been developed to maximise the views across the water so that the rear aspect had large expanses of glass in the three-story structure. These required a specialist window cleaning service to reach the highest points, and a single company had the contracts to fulfil this, and regular personnel were employed to do this.

It becomes human nature to enquire of the individuals who visit on a regular contracted day, for neighbours to seek any information about others, especially the secretive two at number 10. It was reported that on the days cleaning was due all the internal blinds would be closed, but it was on the day the contractors turned up a day early and unexpectantly that the mystery of number 10 was solved.

The window cleaners on their way out of the Vale reported to the security guards that they had seen each and every bedroom to have a themed existence; some they said contained what looked like S & M equipment.

The security guards had already become suspicious from the number and different vehicles pulling up at the guard house to ask for directions to number 10. The latest information courtesy from the window cleaners confirmed that number 10 was no normal residence.

In the Abbey, one of the apartments was occupied by the Chief Police Superintendent from Chester. Once the guards had been alerted to the discovery, the Chief Superintendent was stopped on his way home and informed of the situation.

Two days later, a police raid at number 10 discovered that it was in fact being used as a high-class house of entertainment for business men from Manchester, who had wanted a place remote from their locality for greater discretion. The lady who had bought the house from James was the brothel owner and the two residents were young women from the Ukraine, specially chosen for their skills and good looks.

The police were quick to close the operation down so once again number 10 was up for sale only one year after James had left.

Although James had obtained a good price the year before, the consequent redecoration of the house no longer made it an easy place to sell and as it was seen as an asset of criminal activity. it had been seized by the authorities and put up for auction.

Here again was a deemed high value property in danger of being sold at a price not reflecting its true value. The residents of Wyrevale still reeling from the low price sale of the former house of Siobhan and Patrick and now occupied by Greg and Julia, were again on tenterhooks as to the investment decision they had made.

As the repossession of the house had been made by the police in Manchester, the auction was held at Gascoigne Halman in Wilmslow, who dealt with property in south Manchester and North-East Cheshire, although not in their usual sales area, the house on the Lakes was given to them to sell nevertheless. They set a reserve price of £700,000 reflecting the necessary work to be done to restore the building to a domestic setting.

The auction was advertised throughout.

Manchester and Cheshire and set for late September. George with his usual curiosity of prices in the locality was on the case and realising that here was an opportunity to purchase a property on the Vale at a bargain price, obtained all the details and arranged a viewing.

It was clear on entering that the bedrooms, for every room apart from the kitchen and a small bar, were themed rooms of entertainment.   The   property   had conventionally five bedrooms with three on the first floor with their en-suite facilities and two more with a bathroom between them on the second story. The ground floor study and dining room had been converted too.

It had been maintained well as the clientele were high worth individuals and would have expected no less. £2000 a night had included champagne from the well-stocked bar and large American fridge had been kept full of caviar. But George, using his long-held knowledge of property conversion, it had been a second bow to his business career, estimated that at least £150,000 would need to be spent on its restoration to normality. The reserve price in his opinion had been set too high and although James had received £850,000 the year before, properties of this type were generally exchanged for £650,000.

The auction failed to reach its reserve and the property was to remain vacant for many months.

Chapter Five

Scandal, What Scandal

Scandal what scandal!

A brothel on the Vale and on the Lakes too, considered by many of the residents of that hamlet, second only to the prestigious homes on the Views, the prime location, although residents of Devils Rise would dispute this.

The conspiracy theorists saw this as a revenge plot designed by James to compensate for what he had decided was mistreatment by the local society and the bitter feelings kept from Paula's departure.

It is a funny old world where the public outrage that can be generated by the discovery of such an enterprise in their midst, is not always a reflection of the individual's personal background.

Jez and Megan had survived the Inland Revenue Enquiry by the skin of their teeth. Only an arrangement funded by some very dodgy money had dealt with this.

Megan had been fully aware of the background to Jez and his rise from amateur boxer to health club entrepreneur for it was her company that had sanitised his history in the first Megan had begun life as Megan Rhys-Jones in the seaside town of Rhyl in North Wales, being sufficiently close to the cities of Liverpool and Manchester to make it a popular holiday resort.

Her parents ran a Seafront concession selling souvenirs, beech accessories and ice cream. Although the season was short, May to September at the most, in the 1950's before mass air travel and England was emerging from the austerity of WW11, they were able to make a decent living from the substantial number of holidaymakers.

Megan, who by 1962 had reached the age of seventeen, had been given the opportunity through her good A-Level results to attend University. She had applied to Manchester, Birmingham and UCL in London to study Business, but wanted dearly to be accepted by UCL to take a break from what she perceived to be the doldrums of the North Wales Coast.

It was the beginning of the swinging sixties and although the emergence of Merseyside spawning not only the Beatles but others too. The Searchers, the Hollies, the Fourmost, the Merseybeats, the Swinging Blue Jeans, and Gerry Marsden it was still a local scene. It was necessary to be in London to take part in the Carnaby Street experience.

Despite receiving a grant towards her University fees from her local authority, the means evaluation of her parents reduced that sum considerably. Her Father did not appreciate that he should make up the difference until a year after she graduated. Megan was thus short of funds and London was and still is much more expensive that Rhyl even then.

The small supplement her Father gave her was swallowed up by living expenses, so if

Megan wanted to enjoy the very active social life, she needed an additional source of income. At this stage, she realised that her course was not for her and switched to an English Degree.

Hugh Hefner had set up the Playboy Empire in the United States and opened a club in London in 1960 in Mayfair. The trademark hostesses known as Bunny Girls for their provocative costumes, complete with tails and ears, were recruited locally.

Megan was an attractive blonde with an excellent figure. The opportunities and the sums to be made was passed from a fellow classmate who had applied for a position. She passed the interview and entered the training programme.

The Playboy Club catered for high rollers in the London Scene and attracted a large number of the criminal underworld. Jez whose boxing career had come to an end had taken a position of minder to one of the lesser-known players, who nevertheless was sufficiently funded to regularly play the casino in the Club.

Megan, acting now as a fully-fledged Bunny Girl and hostess to the players in the casino, would serve drinks at the gaming tables. High Rollers got their drinks subsidised by the management, but their entourage still had to pay full price. Jez in his position of minder and in the light of his past training was not one for large amounts of alcohol and certainly not whilst working, for he needed to be alert at all times.

Megan would pass by the tall handsome stranger on her way to and from the bar. She was attracted to him, but the strict Bunny Girl rules did not allow her to stop and chat.

These first contacts would be remembered years later when both of them had risen through their own successful companies, but only by Megan who had a photographic memory.

In the two years post-graduation, touring the world as a purser on cruise ships, she was to meet a number of successful individuals, especially during formal dining evenings.

On one such occasion, her table guests included a couple who had a successful PR company, and a baker and his wife. From the conversations, she gained sufficient insight in PR that it triggered a desire to move her career in that direction.

Returning to the UK, she put herself through an MBA course in business management and sought a position in the PR industry, gaining sufficient knowledge and contacts to begin her own company within three years.

Jez stayed a minder until the death of his Father when he inherited the boxing gym in the East End. The Club had been in the family since the 1930's for the East End was known to be a rich breeding ground for professional boxers who came up from the amateur rings. Boxing was popular with many young lads who saw it as a way out of the poverty that existed there.

As a young boy, Jez too had experienced these same feelings especially in his teenage years, however the Golden Horizon is more often than not never reached. The pot of gold at the end of the rainbow moves away with every step towards it.

In the 1970's the steady climb in national wealth, never more clearly shown than the rise in continental holidays, with the beaches of the Mediterranean attracting people who wanted to look good in their bikini's and tight swimwear, fuelled the health style movement. Jez was quick to realise that here was an opportunity to expand the use of his gym and those seven neighbouring ones he had bought into his stable, in the leisure business and body beautiful, now considered de rigueur. He formed Shire Leisure in 1975 with six venues in East London and Essex.

As the years progressed, increasing numbers of areas of the country were open to the expansion of his business and he was planning a Stock Market launch to fund the expansion of the company. To do this he needed not only a sale brochure but also a clean break from his past background with a story that would be accepted by the institutions who were likely to promote his shares on the floor of the Exchange.

Megan's company would do that for him. She ran her office from a first-floor premises off Oxford Street near to St Christopher's place with its multi-ethnic restaurants. Jez would turn up one day with the request for promotion and sanitation.

Megan recognised him from years past and the story he wished to be hidden confirmed that this was the handsome guy from her youth and time spent at the Playboy club. The sanitisation was necessary, for Jez had used his underworld connections to fund the early expansion of his business, and not always in ways that used laundered money, for he was known for his strong-arm tactics in purchase negotiations. In particular his expansion into Essex away from his natural territory. At that time, institutional money was not available to him with his background, too well known in the East End.

Criminal activity can generate vast amounts of cash that has to be carefully laundered through legitimate businesses. Jez gave his connections the opportunity to use his company in this way, in return for which he paid a price. To aid in disguising the source of his backers, Megan had set up on offshore company.

Money deposited on Islands in the Caribbean and Central American companies would allow any attempt to trace the money route more difficult. An investor would buy shares in the company and receive dividends on those shares which would be reinvested in another offshore site. Final dividends declared in favour of Shire Leisure would fuel the expansion in the UK.

The Nutritional Company that the Inland Revenue had been so intensely interested in, had been one of the companies held on the British Virgin Islands. This had provided Jez with a tax-free income or so he thought but later events would prove that to be wrong.

Megan's promotional literature for the new Shire Health and Leisure Group held information to the effect that a group of companies based in the West Indies were keen to invest in the expansion of Shire, providing a sum of £10,000,000 in 1995. Whilst she and Jez were working together, the constant connection fuelled the pilot light of their relationship.

Jez expanded from Essex into East Anglia and with that move he and Megan bought a seven-bedroom mansion in the small village of Sandon. This was conveniently placed for a quick return to Liverpool Street in London and enabled him to keep contact with his business interests in the capital. In so doing he did not completely break the contact with his roots and his connection with the criminal underworld in that part of the city.

Jez's Father and his boxing gym had provided much of the muscle for the gangs that had followed the end of the second world war and, in his child-hood was familiar with many of the dangerous individuals who had survived and thrived in the late 1950's and early 60's.

Following his Father's death and the inheritance of the gym, Jez had not lost that connection and used it in his early years in charge, to grow the company to seven local facilities in and around the capital.

It became obvious to him in the 1970's that the influence once held by the gangs of yesteryear was fading in the intense police activity to eradicate the criminal underworld, and as he was a former athlete himself, he was not enamoured by the increasing drug trade and its connection cartels. It was time to become legit and the growth in leisure clubs gave him that opportunity but without the help of Megan and her PR company this would have been much more difficult.

Once he had achieved the growth to 25 sites in 2004, it was time to retire, and he sold the company at age 55 to a Capital Wealth Fund from the Middle east. The funds, £25,000,000, were sufficient for both he and Megan to retire with her disposal of her company too. It was also time to break that link with the East End and the proximity of Wyrevale to North Wales and Megan's home base, made the purchase of the house in Devils Rise an escape route.

Jez had employed Knight Frank, one of the UK's leading independent real estate consultancies to seek a suitable home for them within easy striking distance of the North wales coast and had been recommended to Wyrevale.

Purchasing the property on Devils Rise, they had been one of the first residents of this prestigious development and had been able to select the plot with the best view down the valley to the Welsh hills beyond. Megan became a lady of leisure and would form the ladies who lunch group, whilst Jez returned to his favourite hobby, a collection of motorcycles. From Wyrevale he had the empty roads of North wales to ride.

The grey beard and pony tail were to follow now that the boardroom no longer required him to be suitably coiffed and dressed. Megan and Jez thus became a retired couple confidently well off and if a little eccentric in their dress and interests, stalwarts of the neighbourhood. No one would guess the origins of that wealth and any enquiry would be dealt with by Megan's former colleagues in the PR company.

The Inland Revenue enquiry was a shock. Little had he expected that he would need the help from down south to deal with HMRC, many years after his attempt to put his past behind him.

The sale of his business and that of Megan's PR company had provided them with wealth sufficient to take that early retirement but this was held offshore as a consequence of Megan's activity to sanitise Jez's background. It could not easily be reached in large sums without attracting interest of the Authorities. Given that HMRC had given him 7 days to pay the £1.5 million tax liability, he had resorted to his contacts in London to fund it.

They knew he was good for the return but still insisted on a steep rate of interest which would tie him in with them for several years to come as he recovered his money in small amounts from the Caribbean.

All of this was held secret from the social group who were only aware that he and Megan had begun to take several holidays a year in the Leeward Islands. Little did they know that from there Jez could take discreet trips to Tortola and St Vincent where his money was held.

On St Vincent in particular he had contact with the local drug lords who were running cocaine from Venezuela, those 75 nautical miles away across the azure blue seas. This had made that Island relatively prosperous during times of depression, but no one asked the question why. They had been part of the first funding growth of his leisure business allowing him to launder their ill-gotten gains through a company on Tortola.

Chapter Six

Criminal Activity

Criminal activity was no stranger to Wyrevale and with Jez's long held secret background and the activity surrounding Patrick and Siobhan's departure, it was not unknown to discover that former residents were suspects too.

On its start in the late 1980's Wyrevale had struggled to sell the concept so for many years after the construction of the peripheral road, no properties were built. The original developer sold out to a new nationwide company who in the late 1990's saw an opportunity to begin development with the rise in national wealth.

The show houses were built in Brookdale, close to the Abbey and alongside the stream which tumbled down the hillside and had been the source of the site when the Abbey was first built in AD 1242. The hamlet was the first to be developed en masse though selected plots were to be built to order on Devils Rise. Jez and Megan were one of the first to take that up.

The stream meandered its way down to the Lakes alongside the peripheral road near to the entrance and the future gated entry. The residents of Brookdale, the first occupants were to begin their occupation in late 2000 and early 2001, following a drastic cut in the price that was being asked for those properties. Amongst these were a couple who had plain wealth in spades.

Material demonstration of clear wealth can usually be seen in the quality of vehicles parked in the driveway. Here was a silver Mercedes M-class for the wife and a royal blue Porsche 911 cabriolet for the husband. He was quite often missing for several days at a time.

Wyrevale had attracted many of the new breed of technology entrepreneurs and mobile phone company execs. It was known that the couple at number 7 Brookdale had mobile phone connections, but they kept themselves to themselves. Although one of the first tranche of residents, they did not join the group that formed the fledgling Residents Society, from where the social groups emerged.

Being not uncommon to not see the husband for several days, it became clear that he had not been around for a while and the 911 had been missing for a few weeks. The silver Mercedes was seen to go and come back, but he was never in it.

Local gossip is always rife in a tight community like Wyrevale was becoming, and it was suggested more in jest than anything, that maybe he was in prison, for no knowledge to that effect existed.

It was Roger who on reading national press reports, discovered that a mobile phone scam involving unpaid VAT, was being pursued in Holland and a large player had been arrested there for running this scam on the Costa del Sol. The arrest warrants had been issued Europe wide.

People connected to the arrested individual were followed, upon which the resident at number 7 had been stopped in his 911 in Northern France in an attempt to return to the UK and transferred to Holland for trial. He was given a two years gaol sentence to be served in the Netherlands.

Number 7 was vacated and sold, and no one knew where the wife went. Some eighteen months later, the wife was seen again this time in a red Audi convertible, and this time she was looking to buy a house on the Lakes. When the sale was completed several days after. she accepted residence again. Her husband re-appeared this time driving a Porsche Cayenne Turbo in silver with red Brembo brakes. Having spent the last eighteen months ensconced in gaol in Holland, he could not have been earning money to allow for both the house purchase and the £90,000 Porsche.

Crime they say does not pay but it would appear that if you manage to salt away the money before you are caught then it is still there when released early for good behaviour.

They occupied the Lakes house for two more years following his release but as before they were soon to leave and not return. It was not known whether further criminal activity had stimulated this second disappearance.

—

With the growth of mobile telephone use and the much-wanted accessories to those handsets, several individuals had seen the opportunity of a quick buck in this field.

One such was Andrew and his wife Sylvia. They had bought one of the original show houses, the biggest of the group built on Brookdale but reflected the larger houses that could be purchased in the other hamlets. The show house was used to sell plots in Devils Rise and the Lakes off plan.

Andrew had worked for a mobile entrepreneur in the 1990's and had proved himself as one of the top salesmen in that company. He had a way with words but could come across as quite arrogant.

Sylvia had been married before and was 10 years older than Andrew and had two daughters by her previous husband. She had her own company and was a main distributor for a beauty product company with a franchise across North Wales and the Northwest of England.

Andrew who believed that his skills as a salesman were too good to be working for someone else's benefit, decided to set up his own company selling handsets and contracts on commission from the network providers, Orange, Vodafone and BT.

His start-up company expanded rapidly for this was the time that the network providers were not selling direct to the users. Andrew would approach companies with multiple mobile phones and considerable usage and offer them better deals.

The service offered would seem to be attractive at the outset, but his contracts had hidden costs in the small print. It would take a very astute financial controller to discover these.

Success continued for a number of years and the apparent wealth created would be reflected in his change to more exotic cars in the driveway, Mercedes ML to Porsche Cayenne for Sylvia, Porsche 911 to Bentley GTC for Andrew.

Several house changes getting bigger and better each time, until there was no longer a house to satisfy his demand on the Vale, prompting a move away to location some 10 miles away with its own land.

The last house on the Vale had been situated on the peninsula of land that drove the fourteenth fairway between the two lakes, with its bridge where the stream joined them. The house, set back from the bridge thus commanded a view of both the upper and lower lakes and was considered the best plot on the Lakes hamlet.

Whilst these moves took him away from the Vale, his presence was always there in the Golf Club, for the house at number 14 (on the 14th fairway) was from where he had developed his network of connections to companies.

To have been able to fund the property off the Vale and not sell number 14 reflected the clear wealth they had achieved from the telecommunication boom.

Rumours, however, began to circulate amongst the social group, led by George from his weekly visits to Rightmove.com, that all was not well for he had noticed that the rural property was now on the market, and Sylvia's beauty franchise had been sold.

It was discovered that Andrew and Sylvia were now living in Chester at a much smaller location, and presumably the tenants at number 14 had a long-term contract on that property which was not available for them to return. In time, some two years later, they were to reappear at number 14, but no Bentley and no Mercedes. Sylvia was driving a two-year-old Audi A6 estate and Andrew, leather clad, a pale green Kawasaki Ninja 650.

One company, who he had sourced through the club, used 50 handsets on their sales fleet. Their maintenance contracts had begun to rise with increasing complexity of the smartphones available as the Blackberry handsets allowed them more email contact with salesmen on the road.

Andrew at the outset, offered this company a contract at what appeared to be very competitive rates, but little did he realise that the company Financial Officer was scrutinising every invoice that came in for his costs had been rising unexpectantly. The company was a big player in the local Chamber of Commerce and began to ask others about the practices of Andrew's company. When alerted to this, it was found that the overcharging was wide-spread and not simply found within the investigation.

When challenged, Andrew had no ground to stand on other than it was in the contracts signed by each admittedly buried in the small print. He lost several big contracts overnight and his reputation was severely damaged.

The original real move from Wyrevale was prompted by this fall from grace. The return heralded an end to their companies, and the house was marketed and sold from where they were not seen again on the Vale, having been dropped by all their contacts there through their shady dealings.

Jack and Rebecca (Becky) had bought one of the first houses to be released on the Lakes, situated with its back garden overlooking the green of the par three 13th hole. As one of the early residents, they had joined the fledgling social group and were fully committed to the rise of the Residents Society. It was not clear what Jack did, but he had a company based in Altrincham, south Manchester, in tele-communications and would make the daily 30-mile journey to and from in the black, personalised number plate carrying (T313 COM) Audi A8.

It was noted that following the publicity and the court cases in Holland, placing an earlier resident firmly ensconced in a gaol in the Netherlands, that the Audi was conspicuous by its presence in the driveway from day to day. Jack was no longer making his daily work trips, and Becky had downgraded her white Audi Q3 for a Mazda MX5 in red. They had no children.

Local gossip wondered how this had come about. Those residents, still in contact with the telecom industry, confirmed that Jack, realising the dangers of the Netherlands' case, as he was teetering on the fringe of legality, had disposed of his company and chose to retire at 42. Their contact with the social group began to dissipate, to a position whereby they were not seen again regularly on the Friday night Golf club meets.

It became clear to the social group that they did not fully know their neighbours.

Chapter Seven

Vacant property

A bright orange Land Rover Discovery, of dubious age, for it carried the number plate M43VES, and complete with air-intake snorkel and Camel cigarette logos, pulled up at the security gate to ask the direction of the guards for the property at number 10 the Lakes. The guards new that this property had been vacant since the failed auction the year previously and had become quite an eyesore in that hamlet. Neighbouring households had made many attempts to get the authorities to act on its disposal and hopefully restoration, without success.

In its previous illegal possession, the guards were more akin to directing Jaguars, Mercedes and Bentleys to number 10, even though their suspicions made that a dubious activity. To be asked this day, by the occupants of this curious vehicle, with strong Irish accents, the same question again, concerned them. Nevertheless, their duty fulfilled, the Land Rover left for its half mile journey, turning left on the peripheral road, conveying the occupants and two large Rhodesian Ridgebacks to their destination. The occupants of the Land Rover were Tadhg and Maeve O'Kelly.

They were of traveller stock but had decided to give up their natural roaming of the country and make a permanent home. They had come across the failed auction of number 10 and had offered to take the property in its current condition for £450,000 cash. The authorities were all too ready to dispose of this house as it had become an eye sore and the number of complaints from other residents on the Lakes was increasing daily.

It was not known to the neighbours at 12 and 8 that this property had been sold and the attention drawn by the bright orange vehicle in the driveway, would yet again stimulate the gossip machine.

Who were these people, for in their dress sense and outward appearance they were not the typical occupants of a house on the Lakes. It was felt that this occupation, if that what it was, would be a down grading of their surroundings.

Although Tadhg and his wife kept themselves very much to themselves, they became the curiosity of the resident social membership, in the Golf Club Bar. Tadhg in particular was a regular there. Maeve was more often seen leaving the Vale, cigarette firmly clamped in her mouth, smoke pouring from the half open driver's window of the Discovery. Tadhg had brought along his Nissan Navarra pickup truck, complete with tow bar of their earlier life. Neither vehicle was ever considered clean.

Primitive improvements could be seen in the garden with the long grass and weeds cut down by a very noisy petrol driven brush cutter early one Sunday morning.

Normally a sleepy place to live, it was one of the attractions of the plots on the Lakes, the noise disturbed the peace.

Many a neighbour, anxious for a Sunday morning, relaxing in bed with the Sunday Times, was irritated by this intrusion. They were grateful that the eye sore had been improved but would have preferred it to have been done at some other time.

The front of the house now looked much better, but the presence of the two large dogs did not do much for the sight at the back. Dog fouling on the Vale was a subject constantly visited by the management company, in its monthly newsletter, with all dogs to be kept on leads and excrement to be deposited in the bins provided along the peripheral road.

Tadhg in his earlier life had had no such restrictions and seemed to be oblivious or didn't care of the niceties required by residents. His dogs were left to occupy the back of the house, fouling and barking day and night, and when taken away from the house were never restrained by leads. Ridgebacks are big dogs and originally bred in South Africa for the hunting of lions, who would keep the animal's attention whilst their owner lined up the shot. To see these, obviously bred for their aggressiveness, loose on the Vale was disturbing for those neighbours, particularly the ones with small children.

Complaints were laid with the management company and Tadhg and Maeve were asked to obey the covenants attached to their house. Little changed. Why would it for they both seemed to ignore actions of decent behaviour.

Tadhg would be absent for many days at a time, leaving Maeve alone with the dogs with whom she was not seen outside of the property. It seemed that only Tadhg had control of them.

Each hamlet had its own street lighting, with the peripheral road in darkness between each. It became clear that when Tadhg was in residence, he began to walk the dogs late at night, presumably to avoid being seen and therefore not complained about.

Alex and Joan lived on the Lakes at number 8.

One night they had arrived back from holiday at 2am on Friday/Saturday morning, from their villa in southern Spain. Alex on closing the shutters to his master bedroom was to see Tadhg, dogs loose before him, making his way along the peripheral road, back to number 10, and by the way he was weaving, after his heavy drinking at the Golf Club Bar. He had thus taken a complete circular route around the lower lake and must have used the fourteenth fairway to complete that, even when sober this would be difficult in the dark.

No one was supposed to use the golf course as a foot path, and the prospect of dogs fouling the course was a ban on dogs on the greens and fairways. Tadhg, at night had used the expanse of grass as a natural toilet for his animals.

More letters would be sent to the management company and further rebukes would arrive at number 10. The neighbours were further worried by the arrival of building contractors who went ahead to extend number 10 towards the Lake which required the felling of numerous trees which formed part of the landscaping.

When complaints again arrived at the management office, it was to their surprise that these events were taking place as no request for permission had been received. It was a part of the covenants that the management as well as the local authority permission was needed to change the buildings.

Once the authorities had been alerted, Tadhg was not seen again, but for 3 months the orange land rover would appear at weekends with just Maeve on board. The dogs had gone too. It was assumed they had returned to Ireland. After that first period no one was seen again at number 10 and the property remained empty. The gardens again fell in disrepair.

George yet again took an interest in this property as he thought that now an investment here was a ripe opportunity to make some money. He sought details from the agents, Reeds Rains, with whom the property had now been placed by bailiffs as it turned out, that Tadhg and Maeve had left large debts in place after their disappearance.

He ventured to look at the house, armed with his camera. to find that not only had the place not been redecorated from its earlier house of entertainment but now the whole interior had been devastated. The pictures he took were to shock the neighbours. All cabinets in the kitchen had been ripped out, the bathrooms trashed, and the light fittings pulled from the ceilings. The building work was incomplete so adding this to his original estimate at the earlier vacancy, the £150,000 was now considerably short of the required funds. His interest was not fulfilled.

The house would remain vacant for a further two years.

Chapter Eight

The Abbey and Return of Tony

The development of Wyrevale had begun in the late 1980's but had been postponed for more than fifteen years when the housing boom collapsed. The original developers were no longer in a position to create their design, having bought the Abbey and its grounds from the estate of the deceased previous owner.

The Abbey dated back to the 12th Century when it was inhabited by Cistercian monks and survived until closed by Henry VIII in 1534 as part of his dissolution of the monasteries, and part of the buildings were demolished.

There remained however part of the cloisters which were taken over by a local resident and converted into a domestic property. Through various generations, the Abbey was extended and altered with some of the medieval rooms remaining.

In the 16th century it was taken over by a local peer whose whole family supported Charles I in his struggle with the Parliamentarians, during extensive fighting on the locality. Part of the buildings were destroyed during the civil war.

It remained with peer's descendants until the early 1900's when it was acquired by a wealthy shipping magnate from Liverpool who turned it into a fine country house. Following his death in 1935, the house was bought by a local employer for staff accommodation and during WWII was used as a military hospital.

At the end of WWII, the local employer had no further use for it and it was given to the Salvation Army as a home for displaced people. In 1977, the Army could no longer fund the 35-bedroom establishment and it was sold to the first company to develop into a private golf club and apartments.

The outline design for the Golf Course was laid down at this time with much sculpting of the grounds to produce the rise and fall, the lakes and the peripheral road that remains today.

When the second develop took over, they set about changing the direction of some holes, notably the third, sixth and fourteenth, thereby giving more opportunity to build the hamlet design that had been approved by the local planning.

The show houses and the renovated Abbey apartments were available in 2000 and sales were sought. The show houses had been built on the Brookdale hamlet, close to the Abbey so that the marketing suite could deliver not only the potential houses, but also the apartments in the Abbey itself.

The North wing of the Abbey was kept for the Golf Clubhouse, Pro Shop and function rooms, which in future years were made available for private parties and weddings. The Golf Course itself, designed to USPGA standards, would not be mature enough to be played until 2003.

The show houses were built to reflect the properties that would be available in all of the future hamlets, ranging from the small 3-bedroom Brecon design, through Denbigh a four-bedroom detached, to the five and six-bedroom three story houses that would be available on the Views and Devils Rise. These, the Flint and Clwyd would be the most expensive.

The first hamlet to be completed would be Brookdale, but all the hamlets were in progress with the last one to be completed on the lower lake some five years later.

Tony had originally been one of the early residents buying a five-bedroom house on Devil's rise and would be a regular at the Golf Club bar on a Friday night.

Following his divorce from his first wife Charlotte, he and his new partner Maria had bought an apartment in the Abbey, whilst Charlotte kept the house with the children. Such was his wealth from his successful company that neither properties had mortgages against them.

The relationship with Maria failed after five years because Tony needed new excitement and his affair with Susie had been discovered by Charlotte whilst shopping in nearby Sandbach. She was only too pleased to spread the word on the Vale. The fact that Susie looked not dissimilar to Maria was a curiosity that intrigued the group.

Tony had left Maria in the apartment but this time she had to find funds to settle all the debts. She managed this only by mortgaging the apartment and developing a business in nearby Northwich.

Tony did not need or didn't bother to challenge her a part of the funds raised in this way. He left the Vale.

Tony had been a keen golfer and with his 6ft 2in stature and ex-commando figure dutifully maintained by a rigorous exercise regime, had begun to play golf again at Wyrevale. His appearance in the Club House began the gossip again. Now at 65 the silver hair made him look more distinguished and there was no lady present. What had happened to Susie?

Derek, as usual, was the first to try and discover the story behind this new return. Being a regular on the golf course he had ample opportunities to approach Tony at the bar. Welcoming him back he proceeded to ask where had he been for the last few years and why had he come back?

Tony was not surprised to be approached in this manner as he had been familiar with the gossip of his departure and now having returned, he knew that the social groups would begin their interest again.

Tony had spent the last few years on the Island of St Vincent in the Caribbean where had had built himself a villa, six miles north of Kingstown the capital, near Brighton Beach. It was situated on a headland that faced the

Atlantic side with views to Bequia and Mustique beyond.

Tony in his army career had met many young military men who, as an escape from unemployment, for unemployment was high on the Island, obtained a decent job by joining the British Army. This connection had drawn him to the capital Kingstown on one of his leaves from duty.

He had fallen in love with the warmth that people had given to him on his visit and with the success of his venture back in the UK had obtained permission to build his villa.

Of the many Islands in the Grenadine Chain, St Vincent is the largest and most prosperous. It has recorded surpluses on its economy when other Islands, St Lucia and Barbados were suffering a downturn. In this respect, its closeness to Venezuela and Columbia must not go unnoticed, only seventy-five miles across the sea.

The wild, mostly uninhabited west coast was an ideal landing point for the drug couriers in their high-speed cigarette boats, whose cargo would then be onward dispatched to the USA.

Tony, whilst serving in Bosnia, had become friendly with many of the Italian members of the United Nations peacekeeping force, and by chance his friendship with Mario Antoinetta would be rekindled when they met one night in Basils Bar on Bay Street in Kingstown.

Tony became curious as to why Mario was there. Mario explained that when he had left Bosnia, had been discharged from the army on disciplinary grounds.

His name came to the attention of the Ndrangheta in his home city of Reggio Calabria. They knew of his commando training and recruited him as a security advisor.

He was on St Vincent in that role as several shipments from Columbia had gone missing in transit from the Island. It was his job to seek out the culprits and have them "investigated".

Tony had been interested in the money that could be made in that profession and when Mario said that he was working on a commission basis but had always returned six figures in US dollars each year, Tony had become more than interested.

Back in the UK, his wife at that time, Charlotte, was burning through his money rapidly and mainly on alcohol. He was struggling to get his fledgling company off the ground and had recently been turned down for further capital funds.

He suggested to Mario that he might be able to help in their transport department as he regularly shipped goods from the US to the UK in his legitimate business. This could be a new route into Europe for Mario's enterprise.

Mario was not in a position to sanction this, but a senior member of the Ndrangheta was to be present on Antigua in the next few days and if Tony would travel with him, they could arrange a meeting.

On the following Tuesday, Mario and Tony took the LIAT flight to Antigua via Barbados from ET Joshua airport, and met the senior member in St Johns, the Antiguan Capital. Antigua had been an important shipping point for many years and the senior members presence reinforced this.

Tony out-lined his ideas in a meeting held in English Harbour at one of the quayside restaurants, Incanto. The view of this natural harbour was stunning and added to the excitement or was it fear that Tony had felt.

His suggestions were accepted, and he would arrange for his legitimate shipping from the US to aid in their transport to Europe. This early connection had given Tony the funds he needed to enlarge his business in the UK and begin the investment he needed in the emerging technology. Once set up, he closed off the shipping route but maintained contact on a friend basis with Mario.

Derek was to discover that Tony had this Caribbean connection and had taken holidays there for many years whilst still living on Wyrevale. It was to this villa that he and Susie had travelled after his split with Maria. Looking tanned and affluent Tony's excursion there had been good for him.

What Derek did not discover was that Tony had re-established his Mafia connections whilst on the Island, for Mario was now retired there and living on Mustique. Yet again they had met in Basils bar on Bay Street.

His time spent in the last two years had been to establish this reconnection, to see if his retirement could be enhanced by extra funds. Before their trip, Susie had not been aware of Tony's connections and so it was with complete horror and revulsion that she received this information.

It had never occurred to Susie, to ask where all the money which allowed two former partners to remain in properties, had come from.   Susie was very anti-drugs as she had had a younger brother who died of an overdose at age 22.

She was not prepared to accept that Tony was not peddling just transporting which he considered as only a small meddling in the drug trade.

Having been there for only a month she took the next flight out from the newly constructed Argyle International Airport on Caribbean Airlines to New York via Trinidad and from there to London Heathrow with Virgin Atlantic. She and Tony had not met since.

Tony, now back in the UK had taken up temporary living at a hotel near Tarporley and was back to play golf on a course he knew well. He would also be considering buying on the Vale again, but as yet had not found a property to his liking.

Derek of course knew all and rolled off a list of five properties currently available to buy or rent. Tony thanked him for that and re-joined his golfing four, many of whom appeared Italian.

Maria who still lived in the apartment that she had shared with Tony all those years before was informed by Derek at the next Friday drinks event, that he had seen Tony in the club house a few days before.

She had not had a permanent relationship since Tony had left but had joined the circle of ladies led by Frankie who would seek comfort in the bars of Alderley Edge and Knutsford in the hope of meeting Mr Right. More often these meetings would produce a one-night stand and often with much younger male contact, never wholly satisfactory.

Maria had been able, once Tony had left, to put herself through further education and had begun her own interest in the care of the elderly. She had bought a struggling care home in nearby Stoke-on-Trent and had become moderately successful in turning it around to meet all the current legislation and the interest of the Care Quality Commission (CQC).

Such was her success that she was asked by the CQC to take a look at establishments who were on their concerned list, and function as an advisor to the then owners in bringing about the changes that were needed.

The advantages to Maria were that she no longer had to find extra capital for investment and this aspect of her job would lead her away from that care home in Stoke to become a national point of reference, a trouble shooter on call with rescue plans.

The opportunities did arise however to buy the worst of the homes and revitalise them and in so doing she began to build a group business, which became large enough to move away from Northwich and set up a separate headquarters office in Altrincham.

There she employed a staff of twenty-one to manage the homes to her high standards and the company Care-like-Home was born.

She became a woman re-born in her own wealth and no longer needing a man to support her. Her life became a mix of business and international travel and the purchase of a small derelict Chateau in the Charente region of France.

The restoration of this became her hobby and she would spend six weeks at a time in France, with of course daily contact to HQ. Sufficiently close to the airport in Bordeaux, she was only two hours away from Manchester by air should it be necessary.

Maria had been a close friend of Joan when she and Tony had lived in the apartment and this closeness had survived Tony's first departure. Now with her own success and hobby, the skills that Joan had in interior design would be put to use in the Chateau and kindle their relationship.

Now that she was a much more independent woman, she dismissed the return of Tony as an event of the past from which she had successfully survived and had gone forward without a backward glance.

She had taken a residence in London, a first floor 3-bedroom apartment in George Street, Marylebone. Here she would entertain the ladies group on their shopping trips to the capital and overnight stays for the theatre. Joan was a frequent resident.

Chapter Nine

Alex and Joan

Alex's troubled relationship with his brother and the road accident of the latter, had not improved his mental state. The depression he experienced post John's death, had eased after 5 years on the anti-depressant Citalopram and he was under review on a 3-monthly basis with his doctor.

Joan's business had gone from strength to strength, with the rise of internet shopping, she had set up an office and warehouse on the outskirts of Northwich with a staff of five dealing with delivery and dispatch. Her role was changed, from daily hands on, to managerial tasks and released her to devote time to other interests.

The purchase of the derelict Chateau in Charente by her close friend Maria and the latter's request for help on the restoration gave her a new interest to follow. Easily accessed from Manchester Airport to Bordeaux, she and Maria would spend 6 weeks at a time there to oversee the building work.

Maria had employed a local builder, Monsieur Yves to restore the west wing which was in a bad state of repair. Joan, who happened to be fluent in French which she had studied at University and had spent a gap year in Paris before that, was an immense help in this respect.

Joan had met Alex at a University social event in the 1970's when the student's Union was in full swing with rising musical groups. He was not at the University but had access through a student card he held from night classes he was taking in the department of electronic engineering.

At five feet three he was an inch taller than Joan and their respective heights placed them in a standout section of the student population. They had continued their relationship post Joan's graduation and with the then success of Alex's business, Joan had not needed to use her education at that time.

Not one to sit idle, Joan had begun her interest in interior design at this stage and studied correspondence courses at home to extend her knowledge.

About a year before John's death, she had started her small retail business which had moderately sufficient income to maintain them when Alex's depression and the fall in business occurred.

The 1990's saw the rise of the internet and its influence on shopping. Being one of the first to recognise this, Joan's business began to use its influence in the marketplace and very soon her income was outstripping that of Alex.

Alex was a proud man and this further downgrading of his position in their relationship had restarted his depression. At the current doctor review, he explained all this and asked for further help. This came as an increase in the dosage of the anti-depressant.

Their relationship had been struggling for the last ten years, with his libido problem and Joan's occupation with her business growth, had produced a gap between them.

Their communication with each other was almost non-existent and he felt side-lined and even in the marriage, lonely. He needed to feel loved and required an intimacy that no longer existed. He had tried to explain this to Joan, who frankly dismissed his explanations, saying that she no longer wanted his attentions as his failings in the bedroom had not given her any pleasure for a long time.

Now that Joan was helping Maria in France her absence reinforced this loneliness and Alex had resorted to spending many evenings in the club house bar. Sometimes, mainly Friday evenings he would over indulge and his walk back to number 12 the Lakes would be a slow wandering performance.

His route would take him along the footpath separating Brookdale from the third green which was unlit, save for any light from the houses along the way. Many a security light would give him illumination on his way home. Reaching the bridge across the fourteenth fairway gave him access to the Lakes perimeter road and home to number 12. Number 10 was still vacant and deteriorating.

Harriet or Hat as she was known lived at 10 Brookdale, on that side of the bridge over the fourteenth fairway. Her husband had taken a position with Barclays Bank in Abu Dhabi and would spend three months at a time in the Middle East. Her two boys were at boarding school in Shrewsbury, a well-known public school in Shropshire, paid for by the tax-free income her husband obtained.

She too was lonely and had maintained an outside contact with the Friday night attendees at the clubhouse bar. Blonde with a trim figure, she was not unattractive in her late forties. Alex had met her at the bar, and they had a joint interest in being separated from their respective spouses.

One Friday, an occasion when Alex had moderated his drinking, Hat had not. She was very loud and causing some concern in the bar amongst the regulars there. Alex who would have to pass her house on his way home offered to escort her back to Brookdale as he would be going that way.

Slowly, supporting her with his arm around her, they made their way to number 10. At the door Alex asked her for her key and led her into the house as he was concerned for her safety. He decided to make sure she got upstairs and would be secure in her bedroom.

By this time the fresh air and the half mile walk had sobered up Hat for she asked Alex to stay. This took him by surprise but his absent wife gave him an opportunity to be accept. He did fear that his past bedroom performances could be embarrassing.

Hat used the bathroom and appeared in pyjamas giving a signal that it was just company she wanted and had no intentions of any physical contact. Alex who was there by chance had no such night wear and entered the bed naked.

In the morning, much to his surprise Alex woke with an erection which he had not seen in many a year, because of his disfunction. Hat was turning in her sleep and her arm was across his body so he couldn't move.

As she slowly woke, head pounding she became aware of his excitement and took hold. Alex was tingling all over. She gently stroked and lowered her head to take him.

The pyjamas did not stay long and for the first time in 10 years, Alex was not premature in his climax. Both experiencing this together. The mutual intimacy had filled a hole in their respective relationships.

The affair would continue, and it was obvious to the social Friday night that this was happening when their spouses were away, Alex and Hat would attend social events together as a couple.

—

The restoration of the Chateau was progressing well. The six bedrooms had had en-suite facilities added and the four reception rooms were ready for furnishings. A new kitchen would be needed, and the stable block was still to receive attention.

Maria had found a craftsman to restore the grand staircase, which lead from the entrance hall to the first and second floors. She had developed one of the smaller reception rooms into an office from where she could check her business interests in the UK. Joan would use this for her contacts too.

The original landscaping of the grounds had not been lost during the properties decline. Maria had Henri the gardener bring it back to life, adding an outdoor swimming pool off the back terrace next to the stables which were to be used as changing rooms, sauna, and spa.

She had in mind using the property not only as a personal retreat, but also to be hired out as a holiday business. In this respect, the second half of the stables were converted into staff accommodation, for she would need a cook and chambermaids to run the place when hired out, and to make her own use more comfortable.

Joan had been a tremendous help in advising on décor and furnishings and their friendship had grown accordingly. She and Maria would spend many holidays there without male company, it becoming apparent that their relationship had matured into the late realisation that they were attracted more to women than men and had become a couple in France but reserved in the UK.

This realisation explained the many failures that Maria had in that period after Tony and the unfulfilled one-night stands. Joan wondered if her leanings had anything to do with Alex's problems in the bedroom.

When Joan would return to the UK, she and Alex would appear together, but it was plain to see that they were there purely as a pretence of normality.

Maria had no such problems as she had no relationships in the UK and her international life, with different partners, but mainly women, was regularly recorded on social media platforms. Although Joan did not like this, it was necessary to hide their French adventures.

The Chateau was available to hire once completed and with its six bedrooms and on-site staff attracted interest from the attendees at the clubhouse.

Jez and Megan were keen on French holidays after selling the villa on the Costa del Sol, and had toured the country using Megan's XK Jaguar, an indulgence to match Jez's Harley Davidson obsession. The British racing green convertible was an ideal grand tourer with its pace and grace on the uncluttered roads of rural France.

Maria had agreed a discounted price for them in July before the crowds of the French annual holidays in August. They had invited old friends from London to join them and fill the six bedrooms. These were contacts that Jez had kept in the East End and the holiday was a thank you for their help with HMRC, for he had finally paid them off with all the interest.

The Flights were booked from Gatwick airport for their colleagues, and they flew from Manchester to Bordeaux themselves. Two people carriers, Renault Espace, had been pre-booked at the airport to transfer them to the Chateau.

On arrival they were greeted by the Housekeeper Madam Destang and shown to their rooms. Jez and Megan, because they had booked the holiday had the pick of the main Master Suite, with its view of the terrace and landscaped rear gardens, but as the Chateau was set in 15 acres of land carved from the pine forest, all the guests had delightful bedroom views.

The flights had arrived after lunch and the journey from the airport of just over an hour, made their arrival time late afternoon. Madame Destang announced that dinner would be served at 8pm but afternoon tea could be arranged on the terrace.

Temperatures were in the high 30's centigrade and many took immediate advantage of the swimming pool, relieving the travel stress and cooling down before tea.

The service of tea was prompt and held the reputation for pastries, much to everyone's pleasure as lunch had been missed.

The reunion of Jez and his friends from the East End allowed much reminiscing of their dealings in the past, legal and illegal. Jez had long given up such activities and he was surprised to hear that the old-style actions of his friends were now side-lined by the influx of foreign operators and mainly in drugs.

They commented that though in their early days, violence was not ruled out, it was nothing compared to the current level amongst rival drug operations.

Some of the group tried to persuade Jez to join them on new ventures but Megan had taken a strong position and asked him not to get involved. She had enough stress with the recent HMRC enquiry.

The holiday completed all returned home and Megan was able to compliment Maria on her restoration, who responded that much credit was due to Joan's talent. The compliments were more than that of a business colleague which raised comments amongst the social group. Was there something between them?

Chapter Ten

Number Ten, The Lakes

Number Ten, The Lakes had now been vacant for more than two years and despite all the complaints levied with the Management company by Alex and Joan and the neighbours on the other side at number 8, nothing had been done.

The residents at number 8, Craig and Karen had for many years kept themselves very much to themselves and had not been members of the Friday night social group. Their common interest in the restoration of number ten had drawn them closer to Alex and Joan during this period and the four would be seen dining together in local restaurants, and in particular they used the Smoker on the A556 for its quality menu.

The four were aware now, that George had looked at the house as a potential investment, but his pictures of the interior confirmed the damage done, when the Irish previous owners, had departed. It was known too that Claire and Richard, who held a considerable property portfolio, and even with their considerable wealth, had decided too much needed to be spent in restoration.

The further problems to overcome were the lack of approval, from the management company, for the uncomplete building work, and the absence of any planning application for this.

Tony's reappearance in the Clubhouse and conversations with Derek, had stimulated his interest in number 10, as he was now looking to come back to the Vale. He knew that there were problems associated with this property, for why had it stood vacant for so long.

Alex at home alone whilst Joan was in France became aware of the classic E-type Jaguar that arrived next door and was familiar with that car. It must be Tony as the E-type had always attracted attention on the Vale amongst motoring enthusiasts. Alex had a keen interest in motorsport, and the Jaguar XF, which had been upgraded to the R version, that Joan had bought for him, confirmed his dedication to that marque.

When, looking out of the rear bedroom windows, to allow a view over the privacy hedge, he saw the older version of Tony on the over grown terrace. He decided that he would casually be outside when Tony returned to his car.

He had to wait for more than an hour before Tony emerged from the garage to number 10 but was quickly and nonchalantly walking down his drive at that time. Alex had not been close to Tony in his former residency on the Vale, but the E-type gave him an entry into conversation.

The conversation started on the age and version of the E-type, which Tony was proud to say that this was an original mark 1 3.8 litre straight six which he had owned for a number of years.

Alex knew this in any case, but the ice was broken. He followed by asking what was the purpose of Tony's presence as this house had been vacant for so long, and they were joined by Craig who had arrived back from filling his BMW with fuel.

Tony said that he was looking to return to the Vale and had been looking at various properties for sale, and this was one of four that the was considering. Alex and Craig were intrigued as they knew that number 10 did not in any way compare with the other houses available at that time.

Tony cut the conversation short and drove away heading out of the park by the quickest route anti-clockwise on the perimeter road, and cleared the security gate.

Alex and Craig were rooted to the drive as he left and continued a discussion as what was taking place here. They knew that residents with money had looked and left the idea of purchase, but here was an earlier resident returning from a notorious womanising past looking at the house.

During the following four weeks, numerous surveyors and builders would be seen visiting the house, but Tony was not seen during that period.

The covenants of the Vale did not allow for any for sale signs to be displayed so that it was not always obvious when a property had been acquired by a new owner. It was apparent though that movement had occurred in this direction for there was now a permanent presence of builders on site.

Alex was keen to find out what was being done and asked the workmen who was employing them, but all they could tell him was that they were working for a company based in the Caribbean and all instructions came through the selling agent.

The incomplete ground floor extension now contained an indoor swimming pool and games room. A new and expensive Poggenpohl kitchen had been installed, a new staircase added, and a Neville Johnson office provided. All this could be seen by peering through the windows of the ground floor once the builders had left for the day. Both Craig and Alex were updating each other on a daily basis.

The work was completed in six months, and it was clear that a permanent project manager had been appointed to oversee the work for the unknown owner had not appeared.

Joan who had spent most of that summer with Maria in France, returned in the September complete with an overall sun tan. No signs of bikini coverage and an indication that nude sun bathing was possible in the discreet surroundings of the Chateau. Maria had returned to Marylebone in a similar look of health.

Joan had been vaguely aware of the work next door by receiving regular updates from Alex, but those did not fully represent what she saw on her arrival.

The front garden had been cleared, repaved and re-planted. The rear terrace had been extended and the land which fell away to the lake had been newly landscaped with steps leading down to a waterside patio.

Still the owner had not been seen and curiosity was killing not only the neighbours but also the Friday night group.

Alex who with Hat had been attending regularly had kept the gossip going with each weekly update and the fact that no money seemed to be too much to restore that once derelict property. Claire and Richard, Amy and George and others knew only too well the task that had been needed even to return the house to normality, let alone with all the expensive additions.

Late one night in early October, with the night's drawing in Joan was closing the curtains in the front bedroom, which she used as a dressing room, to sort out an evening dress for a coming business dinner in London that she and Maria were to attend.

The headlights of a car pulling into the drive of number ten attracted her attention. It was a Mercedes S-class that she had not seen before. A high-class vehicle with limousine like qualities was being driven by a silver haired figure who was vaguely familiar.

She had not been party to the return of Tony and did not associate this man with the Tony she had known, who had left her partner Maria with all those debts years before. Debts which the independent woman she had become had stimulated Maria's business growth, and their relationship.

Alex in the study, browsing the internet for the latest Formula 1 news heard a car stop close by as the headlight beam had entered his window obstructing the computer screen momentarily. Curiosity took him to the window, and he recognised the new look Tony, emerging from the Mercedes.

Being Friday night, he was to join Hat in the

Clubhouse at 8pm and did he have tales to tell! Much to his despair the group was small that night, no Claire or Richard. No Amy or George just Derek and Michelle and Jez. Megan was visiting her parents in North Wales and the bar was relatively empty.

What a disappointment, his grand revelation did not have the large audience he had expected. However, Derek always keen a recipient of gossip, gave him his full attention whilst Jez was ordering the second round of drinks. Hat and Michelle had drifted off into their conversations.

On Jez's return with two pints of Stella and a Guinness for Alex, he too would join in the inquisition as to how Tony had managed to return and in such a grand manner.

Jez knew, with his underworld connections, that Tony had contacts in the Caribbean, for during one of his money sourcing trips to the Leeward Islands he had seen Tony descending from a Virgin Atlantic 747 at Barbados airport whilst waiting for his own connection to Tortola.

Tony was not alone but accompanied by a very attractive lady of Caribbean origin. Tall and slender her figure, with the classic Caribbean shape, made her stand out from the crowd and the vibrant colours she wore indicated a great deal of self-presence.

Tony and his Lady entered the departure lounge via the in-transit gate and seated for only a few minutes before their flight call to

St. Vincent saw them depart for the LIAT flight of 20 minutes.

They did not acknowledge Jez who was seated some six rows away. This coincidence sparked Jez's mind once Alex had begun his revelation.

Had Tony some mystery wealth which emanated from the sunshine Islands?

His own offshore dealings he knew were secret too, or was this just a holiday visit to the villa that Jez knew he owned on that Island.

There was no way he could offer an explanation to the others of Tony's ability to fund the work without revealing his own past secrets. He was keen however to seek out Tony and discuss matters, of which they may have a mutual interest.

Tony and Simone, his Caribbean partner, would not take up permanent residence in the newly restored house but would be seen to come and go presumably spending the remaining time on St. Vincent, in the villa that Tony had built all those years before.

Simone never came alone, but Tony would make flying, one week stops to address what his neighbours concluded was business meetings in and around Manchester. He remained a closed book, and even when in the Clubhouse on a Friday night drank in his own company whilst watching the in-house tv sports coverage.

The E-type was back and now closeted in the polished floor, centrally heated garage that had been part of the rebuild. Not in regular use for the S-class Mercedes was the day to day transport that Tony used whilst in residence. Only at weekends and in certain warm, dry weather conditions would the Jaguar emerge for Tony's pleasure on the minor roads in and around the hills and mountains of North Wales.

Jez and Megan were scheduled to take one of their regular trips to the Caribbean with the covert visit to Tortola. Jez was keen to investigate whether any of his contacts there knew of Tony and a source of his money.

Offshore Banks are very discreet, and he found it difficult to establish any meaningful contact, but back on St. Vincent where they were staying, Jez set out to discover anything he could about Tony and Simone.

By chance he had sought relief from the mid-day sun in Basils Bar on Bay street beneath the Hotel in which they were staying, to take a spot of Lunch. Seated at the Bar whilst his table was being prepared, he began a conversation with the man sat next to him who was obviously not a native. As usual the conversation began with the question on holidays.

Was he here to enjoy the sunshine?

The response when it came reluctantly was with an accent he identified as Italian. His former contacts in the East End had associated with people who spoke in this way but to discover this, 4500 miles away from Europe was unusual. His curiosity led him to ask, if not on holiday what was he doing here on the Island. The answer he received was that he was a runner.

Marathon or Sprint? Criminal?

Jez explained that he was on holiday but had set out to discover a friend of his who had a villa on the Island, but he was unsure as to the exact location. Did the fellow occupant of the bar know of an Englishman called Tony?

His companion took a step back metaphorically, for here was a man asking after Tony with whom he had regular business. The Italian was Mario, Tony's Island contact. He stated that he had not met any Englishman of that name and excused himself and left the Bar.

The Mitsubishi Shogun left the Bar at speed and headed north towards the new Argyle Airport taking the turning for Brighton Beach and heading out on the headland to Tony's villa.

Tony and Simone were taking lunch by the pool when Mario arrived in a cloud of dust and locked wheels. He hastened to the pool side to tell Tony of his unexplained contact in

Basils Bar. Tony asked him to describe the man at the Bar. Tall, grey hair in a ponytail, London accent he thought and the look from is broken nose of an ex-boxer.

It could not be possible that this was Jez from the UK, but the description was all too familiar.

Why was he here and asking questions?

Jez had told Mario that he was staying at the Cornerstone Hotel on holiday, but Tony doubted that.

Simone had contacts in the hotels of the Island as she ran a travel business in Kingstown. Through these she was able to confirm that an English couple were staying in Kingstown and by chance she was told of a booking at the French Veranda Restaurant in two days for an English couple, for her cousin ran the appointment book at the reception of the Mariners Hotel in which the restaurant was situated. It's a small Island.

Tony, therefore, had the opportunity to investigate by booking a meal at the French Veranda Restaurant to which Simone and he could attend the same day.

The sun sets regularly at 6.30 on St. Vincent and the warm evenings can be pleasantly spent with a cool breeze off the sea.

The French Veranda Restaurant with its position some five yards from the breaking waves and its view across to Young Island is such a place.   The small cocktail bar is welcoming, and the staff are friendly and very attentive.

Tony and Simone arrived at 8.30 taking gin and tonics at the bar. Their meal was booked for 9pm, people eat late in the Caribbean, so clearly positioned they could monitor the comings and goings to the restaurant as the entry was via the bar.

Seated in the left-hand corner beach side, with the gentle lapping sound of the sea in their ears, were Jez and Megan, enjoying the Bresaola and parmesan starters.   Jez was deep in conversation and had not engaged Tony and Simone's arrival.   Tony knew instantly who they were and wondered why they were here and asking for his location.

The owner of the restaurant, a small French woman in her late fifty's, Madame LaFarge, was the front of house this night. She approached Tony to announce his table was ready and with the bottle of wine purchased at the bar, he and Simone descended to sit next to Jez and Megan.

They did this without giving any recognition of their neighbouring table and proceeded to commence the meal they had ordered. Garlic snails for Tony, and a garlic prawn and chilli sauce dish for Simone.

As the next table was being occupied, Megan and Jez stopped their conversation, and both immediately recognised Tony but did not let on. In quiet tones, below the level of the inhouse music, Jez signalled his recognition to Megan who nodded in response. He suggested taking an after-dinner drink in the bar from where he could approach Tony as he left.

Service can be slow in the heat of the Caribbean, and it was some two hours later that Tony and Simone were ready to leave. Jez and Megan were settled in the corner of the bar on the comfortable cushioned rattan furniture, when the couple came into the bar on their way home.

Jez stood and stopped Tony, greeting him as a long-lost friend. Tony pretended not to recognise him at first and only when Jez reminded him of the previous meetings on the Vale, some years before, did he acquiesce in his memory.

He introduced Simone formally as though Jez and Megan would not know her. Taking the position that they would not have known of his purchase on the Lakes.

Jez offered after dinner drinks which Tony accepted but Simone declined. She was tired she said and asked Tony to not stay long and she would call a taxi for her own departure. This was a pre-planned move on their part, with Simone seeking a taxi at reception but discreetly asking the receptionist, who she knew, for details of the guests in the bar.

She discovered that they were not residents and had arrived from Kingstown earlier that evening, confirming yet again Mario's revelations.

Tony accepted an Armagnac from Jez and joined the couple on the seating in the bar corner. Polite conversation followed.

Were they here on holiday?

How long were they staying?

All the usual entrees to be given when people known to you are met in foreign lands.

Jez had decided that this would be more than a casual meeting and stepped in straight away with the statement that they knew he had bought number 10 the Lakes and why, when it was in such a state.

Tony was only too pleased to tell them.

that he had obtained it at a rock bottom price and so could afford to spend a small amount in its restoration.

Small amount!

Jez knew from Alex's updates and constant observation that more than a small amount had been employed to produce the property as it now stood. He therefore continued his quest by asking what he needed to do to bring the house back to normality for he had seen the photographs that George had taken with his first interest.

Tony explained that he had installed a new kitchen, some light fittings and had the house decorated. A friend who was a gardener had tidied the garden for him as a favour. At all times playing down the cost of the rebuild. Jez and Megan knew that this did not equate with the current condition of the house.

Tony was keen to leave and keep his promise to Simone and on standing asked Jez and Megan, as they were here on holiday, whether they were free the following day for he could collect them, and they could lunch at his villa along the coast. The invitation was accepted, and a time and place agreed for a pick-up.

Jez and Megan were left in the bar which was now deserted. The barman asked if they would like a last drink as he was anxious to close for the night. They had much to discuss before retiring so took two more malts from him with the request for a taxi to be called.

They were not staying at the Mariners but had a room at the Cornerstone Hotel above Basils Bar in Kingstown. They would need to ensure that their pick-up the following day was from the Mariners as arranged.

Their taxi driver Crispin transported them back into Kingstown and Jez asked him to collect them from the Cornerstone at 10.30 the following day. They had agreed to be collected by Tony at 12pm.

Deposited at the Mariners at 11am they took a seat on the terrace over-looking the small pool and its view of Young Island. The day was clear not a cloud in the sky, but the cooling breeze was still there from the sea. They watched the yachts leaving the relative calm of the channel between the Islands to enter the Atlantic rollers which were falling further out sea.

They had ordered coffee and a late breakfast keeping the pretence of residents in the hotel.

Tony's Range Rover arrived prompt at 12 and he greeted them again as local inhabitant, inviting new friends to his villa.

The journey along the improved road to the new

Argyle Airport made the journey to the villa one of 10 minutes only, for the Range Rover was an ideal vehicle, smooth and fast on the highway and resilient once taking the small connecting and unpaved road to the headland residence.

Simone was visible on the pool side terrace as they approached and was casually dressed with kimono over her bikini. Jez and Megan were more formally attired although in white jeans and T-shirts still in the holiday mode pretence.

Simone had prepared a salad lunch with deli meats and seafood to be complimented with white wine from Chile, a sauvignon blanc, to be taken pool side under the large green parasol.

Tony guided Jez and Megan past the large Japanese Akai guard dogs that they kept for security in such a remote place, up the six steps to the terrace and there they were greeted by Simone. Lunch was enjoyed and general conversation flowed without hesitation.

Suitably fed it was time to relax and Simone asked Megan if she would like to rest by the pool and could supply swim wear if she so wished. The men declined and Tony asked Jez to join him in the house.

They entered the snug built into the cool lower ground floor and Tony offered Jez a Cuban cigar. Jez, who didn't smoke declined but indicated Tony to take one himself. What a stand off! The six-foot two ex-commando and the still muscled ex-boxer.

Cigar lit; Tony went straight to the point.

Why was Jez asking about him in Kingstown?

Jez was stunned that Tony was aware of this and hesitated in his reply, indicating that he had been caught out.

His reply, when it came was stumbling, not an event for the normally confident ex-boxer. He was there he said because curiosity had driven him to find out the source of Tony's apparent wealth, so many years after his initial departure from the Vale and why had he returned to that derelict property at number ten the Lakes.

To enable the conversation, he had to explain his own connections with the Caribbean and in so doing revealed secrets that no one else on the Vale knew. Tony was intrigued and asked Jez to go deeper and in so doing delaying his own revelations.

Jez admitted that he had considerable funds deposited offshore, which had come from his early life in London, and some if not all, had been derived from dubious activity in his former life immersed in the East End underworld.

Tony got more from Jez than he was prepared to admit himself. He allowed Jez to know that his engineering business, which he had started after his army life ended, had business in the Caribbean in the restoration of old Land Rovers and some small military vehicles. His base had been here in St. Vincent with his employment of ex-soldiers and that is why he was able to build the Villa and seek a residency permit.

From this base his work had spread to the Island chain from Trinidad to Antigua and had been moderately successful, complimenting his work in the UK.

When he diversified into 3D printing in the UK, the engineering side continued here in the Caribbean and had extended beyond the Leeward Islands towards Cuba and Jamaica.

None of this explanation was untrue, except that the restored vehicles carried other cargo undisclosed.

Jez and Megan returned to the UK and at the following Friday gathering were met by the complete social group who were keen for the information they had discovered. Jez gave the explanation that Tony had given with a comment that this could be true, but he had not been able to discover any verification whilst there.

If it were true, and his business was doing that well, then they need not ask any further questions. As they left the Clubhouse most if not all had their doubts.

Chapter Eleven

Christmas approaching

It was six weeks from Christmas and the members of the Clubhouse Friday nights were planning their social events for the holiday periods. The Golf Club held an annual Christmas Ball, but in recent years, the event had been disappointing and once that is in your memory, you are inclined to dismiss this for the current year.

George and Amy were looking for some winter sun and Polly their daughter working for British Airways in Abu Dhabi had arranged flights for them two days before Christmas to stay over the

New Year too.

Lisa, the older daughter, had a New Year break from the BBC when many of the programmes were on repeat and her production role was diminished, was to come for the four days over the New Year.

Lisa had booked rooms for them at the Ritz Carlton, opposite the Grand Mosque and arranged for one of the BA chauffeurs to collect them on time at the international airport, in the company Mercedes.

Claire and Richard had purchased the Villa on La Zagaletta from Jez and Megan and were taking the three children there as soon as the school holidays occurred, to return in time for the January re-start. The winter sun on the Costa del Sol does not compare with the Middle East, but when you have grand facilities that you own, then it makes sense to use them as often as possible.

The out-door pool was heated in any case, and the basement games room, gym and cinema rooms had ample entertainment available should inclement weather occur. They had invited George and Amy, before they realised, they were staying with Polly, and as Nikki was on her own.

Nikki was surprised but grateful for the invitation as to spend that holiday alone is not pleasant. She would of course be returning to Dominica for New Year with her family, so her stay would be a short four days.

Toby, Claire's oldest child was now fifteen and tall like his Father. Richard had encouraged his son to play golf and Toby had obtained a 12 handicap at Wyrevale.

La Zagaletta, with its two Golf Courses, allowed Richard and Toby the ability to play most days, whilst Claire and the twin girls enjoyed the pool and shopping on the coast. Richard and Toby would join them for lunch in one of the quayside restaurants in Puerto Banus.

The children were able to entertain themselves in the evenings, the girls were now thirteen, allowing Claire and Richard to dine out alone. Their favourite venue was El Conte just those few hundred yards left on the main road outside the security gate.

The Friday group remaining in the UK was getting smaller each day, but the party animals were keen to arrange events to enjoy at home.

Jez and Megan were known for their traditional invitation for drinks on the morning of Christmas Day. In the past they would be joined there by Derek and Michelle, Alex, Joan and Maria, Amy and George, Claire and Richard, if they not been away.

Frankie was known to arrive late. Frankie of course no longer lived on the Vale, having left the Lakes after her divorce from Simon, but had maintained her friendship with the group. Much wine would be consumed by the ladies and beer flowed for the men.

The morning would end when people departed around 1.00pm, presumably to sleep off the alcohol before the Turkey was to be removed from the oven if not too over-cooked having been there for several hours in their absence.

Jez and Megan were not around for Megan's parents, this year, had invited them to stay with them in Rhyl, a happening rarely seen before. Maybe with increasing age, her Mother was eighty-six, they believed that this maybe a last time in their lives. Her Father Rhys was still active and at 79 five years younger than his wife, Alwyn, could still hit a golf ball on the nearby Prestatyn Course, with his 18 handicap.

The countryside close by was a familiar playground for Jez on his Harley Davidson and he had persuaded Megan to allow him to bring it along. Megan travelled alone in her Jaguar with the luggage for the holiday.

No Christmas morning drinks party was to be held on Pinewood Close for Jez and Megan that year as no one was around. In many of those away, the idea had become stale in any case.

Boxing day is party day in the household of Colin and Dina as the pair were keen to have as many people as possible to their house, which would be duly decorated and set up with the musical accompaniment on level eleven.

This equipment had the misfortune, for many, of having an in-built Karaoke screen and player. Jez, a regular participant was missing this year, but Dina had invited Michelle and Derek, Alex, Joan and Maria, Michael and Suzanne and Frankie with her friend Sabina.

Sabina and her husband Graham did not live on the Vale. Graham a roofer with his own connections in the building trade, had converted a large derelict farm building in a nearby village some five miles from the Vale. It happened that Sabina was also a cousin of Dina's.

They attended in the large, black, non-too clean Nissan Navarra that Graham used for his company, complete with roofing slates in the back. Why they had not brought Sabina's bright red Audi Q7 was a puzzle.

Sabina was a lady with a large personality. Her died black hair, size 20, five-foot three stature and rich loud language could not be missed. She would consume Prosecco in large amounts and had been a drinking buddy of Siobhan when she was resident on the Vale.

She did however have a good singing voice which was much more pleasant than the out pouring of her usual four-letter words. The voice as such was used extensively once the Karaoke machine was lit up. In this she would be joined by Dina and Derek whose voice would have been better keeping quiet.

Michael was not keen on staying once the singing began and he and Suzanne would excuse themselves early from a party which would normally end around 4am. Their twelve mid-night departure was not missed.

Colin would give his usual burst of George Formby songs on his Ukulele, many of which were new to the younger participants, unless they had been to one of Dina's parties before, for this was an inevitable occurrence. Repetition of such things will eventually lead to non-attendance by the more discerning couples. Same old, same old! Boring!

Frankie, who had many boyfriends (sic) since Simon left with the female Golf Professional, was still attending alone and her personality would rival Sabina much in a quieter, much more refined way. No foul language, slightly moderated tone to her voice but the most out-rage us laugh that was generated by increasing alcohol levels. A real fun time girl. She would not be an early leaver but would not sing.

Frankie was a keen organiser of New Year social years, in getting the Group to attend the Black-Tie event held each year at the Dog and Bone pub in one of the small outlying villages. The event was ticket only and with the diminished Group this year she was only able to book one table for ten. The party consisted of Frankie and new man, Steve. Derek and Michelle, Colin and Dina, Joan, Maria, Alex, and Hat.

Joan and Maria were late additions as Michael and Suzanne had declined the invitation, for Michael had found last year's event too much to handle. Suzanne was disappointed that they were not there but she too recognised that the huge alcohol bill and very loud nature of the party could spoil an evening.

So, the New Year began with a party held locally and others enjoying their Winter Sun not available in North Wales, however.

Tony was still the major topic of conversation.

Printed in Great Britain
by Amazon

27453838R00199